T0105653

Status Quo

Robert Williams Jr.

iUniverse, Inc.
Bloomington

Status Quo

iUniverse books may be ordered through booksellers or by contacting:

iUniverse
1663 Liberty Drive
Bloomington, IN 47403
www.iuniverse.com
1-800-Authors (1-800-288-4677)

Because of the dynamic nature of the Internet, any web addresses or links contained in this book may have changed since publication and may no longer be valid. The views expressed in this work are solely those of the author and do not necessarily reflect the views of the publisher, and the publisher hereby disclaims any responsibility for them.

Any people depicted in stock imagery provided by Thinkstock are models, and such images are being used for illustrative purposes only.

Certain stock imagery © Thinkstock.

ISBN: 978-1-4620-0960-2 (sc)
ISBN: 978-1-4620-0961-9 (ebook)

Printed in the United States of America

iUniverse rev. date: 5/10/2011

CHAPTER ONE

Rhobert's natural mother Ann Rodriguez hated boys. At age three Rhobert was plunged into the foster care system after his mother Ann gave Rhobert up to the Pays des Department of Children Family Services (DCFS) while his father Bob Rodriguez was away serving in the Army. Rhobert's Grandfather on his father's side of the family Owen Rodriguez worked diligently for a whole year trying to get Rhobert's father Bob discharged from the Army for family reasons. After the discharge was granted both Owen and Bob Rodriguez went in search for Rhobert. While in the foster care system for two years Rhobert was shuffled around to four different foster care families. Owen and Bob finally caught up with Rhobert at the fourth foster care family and they took Rhobert home.

Having just been discharged from the Army with nowhere to live, divorced from his wife Ann, Bob and Rhobert moved in with his mother Aline Rodriguez.

Rhobert's Grandmother Aline was recently divorced from Owen. Aline lived alone in a three bedroom apartment in the small quiet little South Western community of Pays des, Illinois. Pays des was named after the historical 17th century French legally undefined region without formal boundaries territory that means Illinois Country.

Bob got himself a job working for his father Owen. Owen owned and ran his own auto body repair shop. Bob soon became a well known expert in the auto body repair business, which was not very hard to do since he was trained at a very young age everything he knew at the business by his father Owen. Bob had one problem though, he loved to drink and he drank every day from morning till night. Bob drank while working and he would drink after work, staying out until the wee hours of the morning. Bob was so good at what he did as an auto body repairman that even with his drinking problem he still managed put out superior quality work. Bob started taking Rhobert to work with him. The garage that Bob worked in was a single story building directly behind a junk yard main office building. Both buildings were surrounded by an old abandoned small creek bed. Some junk was piled up at several locations along the abandoned creek bed, with junk cars stacked up in the parking lot of the main office building and also in a vacant lot across the street of the main building.

When Rhobert was eight years old, one morning his father came home with a girlfriend Ms. Babs Hekate to meet Rhobert and his mother Aline. Rhobert's father announced that he and Babs were going to get married. They also plan to start looking for a place of their own. The very first thing that Rhobert noticed about Babs, but did not say anything was that Babs was a corpulent person and rolled considerably in her gait. Within a week they were married, and within a month Bob and Babs moved out of his mother's house and into their own place taking Rhobert with them.

What started out as simple well deserved discipline, slowly gravitated over time, to outrageous and severe physical, emotional, mental, and sexual abuse. It all started after Rhobert's stepmother Babs gave birth to her children. It was like a day to night change in her from a nice person to an evil person only in regards to Rhobert. She changed to a totally different person with two personalities in what seemed over night.

Rhobert was blamed, and spanked every time one of her children would cry, even if Rhobert was not present, or near them. It seemed that Rhobert was spanked for anything. Babs raised her children to believe that they were better than Rhobert was. Even from an early age they were treated differently, including discipline. Rhobert had rules and breaking them would result in spanking and grounding for punishment.

From an early age Rhobert had to ask for a drink of water, the answer was usually no. Rhobert could not rummage through the refrigerator or the cupboards for food or drink and asking would result in an immediate spanking. Rhobert ate what was put on his plate and asking for more meant spanking. His drink for the meal was always a small cup of water.

Rhobert was only given a bath once a week and Babs would run his bath water for him giving him only one inch of water in the bath tub. Asking for more water in the tub would result in a spanking after. Rhobert could not complain about anything, doing so would result in a spanking.

The normal spanking routine was always in the following manner, and the only change in this routine was that as Rhobert got older more licks and lashes were added on. The spanking routine was always pull down his pants and underwear, grab and hold onto his ankles, and do not let go. Letting go would add at least ten or more lashes onto the total amount that was to be given. The licks and lashes would always be given with a sweeper cord, and if she would hit herself by mistake, then more lashes would be added on. Crying, screaming, begging for mercy had no affect. Sometimes her children were made to watch while Rhobert's punishment was administered. Discipline for her children was totally different. They were never spanked with a sweeper cord, only one or two swats with her hand, if that, with clothes on. They were always punished without emotional or mental abuse.

Every one of Rhobert's spankings would accompany grounding for a minimum of one month. Grounding was confinement to his room, or sometimes locked into the closet in his room. During grounding Rhobert could not go outside, nor could he have anyone come over. If any one did come over, they were rudely turned away.

Rhobert was constantly belittled and berated for anything and everything. He constantly got poor grades on his report card from school which resulted in more punishment. Babs children always received excellent grades on their report cards. It was not until an older age that Rhobert learned Babs was faking and correcting her children's poor grades so that she could show his Dad just how much better that they were than Rhobert was.

One hot summer morning Rhobert was given a very brutal sweeper cord beating. Two hundred lashes with the sweeper cord. His cries for mercy and begging for her to stop to Rhobert seemed to go unheard by her. Unknown to them at the time Rhobert's Uncle by marriage Mr. Ken Shelton is outside working on the Rodriguez's trailer that he was renting to them. Also unknown to Babs, Rhobert was recording the beating on his tape recorder from his bedroom. After the beating, as usual Rhobert would be sent to his room. Rhobert put the cassette recording of the beating in his pocket and while Babs was resting he ran away from home. Rhobert went straight to his Uncle Shelton's house which was two blocks away. Uncle Shelton asked Rhobert, "Just what the hell was that?" "That was me getting a spanking." says Rhobert. "Son look here, that was in no way a spanking. What that was a very cruel and vicious act of abuse that no child deserves to receive. That woman is very sick and deserves to be held accountable for it. Do you understand me? Why haven't you ever come to me about this before?" asks Uncle Shelton. "Because everyone I've ever gone too before, would tell her and ask her about it. She would beat me for telling, so I quit telling anyone because it was useless and all it ever got me was another spanking." says Rhobert. "Does she do that to you all the time, beatings like that?" asks Uncle Shelton. "Yes, that is normal for me to get whipped like that, sometimes on a daily basis and I could not ever tell anyone about the beatings for fear of getting more if she was to find out." replies Rhobert. Rhobert then gave the cassette recording to his Uncle Shelton. "Well it is all over now. You don't ever have to worry about her and those spankings ever again." says Uncle Shelton. Looking at the cassette recording he was holding in his hand, Uncle Shelton says to Rhobert, "I don't need to hear this again, I was there. I will hang on to this for you though." states Uncle Shelton.

Mr. Shelton then goes to the telephone to call the police, when suddenly the phone rings. He picks up the phone to answer it. Rhobert's stepmother Babs is on the other end; and she asks Mr. Shelton, "Have you seen Rhobert?" He yells his response to her on the phone, "Go to Hell lady!" as he slams the receiver down abruptly hanging up the telephone on her. The telephone rings again, and Mr. Shelton answers it. It is Rhobert's stepmother calling again stating, "I am calling the police!" "Call the damned police lady, it saves me a dime!" he shouts his reply to her hanging up the telephone.

The police arrive at Mr. Shelton's house just as soon

after Babs had called them. Police Officer Brice Reid arrives, gets out of his patrol car, and walks up to and knocks on the door. Mr. Shelton tells Rhobert, "Wait here Rhobert, I will take care of this." as he goes to answer the door. Mr. Shelton opens the door and invites Officer Reid in, "Come on in Officer." Officer Reid steps through the door as Mr. Shelton closes the screen door behind him. Officer Reid asks Mr. Shelton, "Mr. Shelton is Rhobert Rodriguez here?" "Yes sir he is here with me." replies Mr. Shelton. "Well Mr. Shelton, I am ordering you release Rhobert you are holding into my custody so that I may take him home." demands Officer Reid. "I am not keeping or holding Rhobert unwillingly. Rhobert is here on his own freewill, and due to cruel and vicious child abuse that he has suffered at home by the hands of his stepmother. And, he does not want to go home, he wants the abuse to stop, and it stops now!" states Mr. Shelton. "What proof of this child abuse do you have?" asks Officer Reid. Mr. Shelton places the cassette recording into the cassette player on the table to let Officer Reid listen to the recording. While listening to Rhobert's beating on the cassette, Rhobert takes off his shirt to show Officer Reid the bruises and the welts. After listening to the recording and wiping the tears from his eyes. Officer Reid calls dispatch requesting that a Counselor from DCFS be immediately made available for Rhobert. As Officer Reid begins to leave he lets Mr. Shelton know, "Mr. Shelton, I am now going to go over to Mrs. Rodriguez's house to inform her she needs to stop harassing you on the telephone. When the DCFS

Counselor is available, I will be back to pick up and take Rhobert to go see her. Also, if you don't mind, I will need Rhobert to take that cassette recording with him." "Yes sir." replies Mr. Shelton. Officer Reid then returns to his patrol car radios in to dispatch and drives off to Mrs. Rodriguez's house. When he arrives at her house he parks his patrol car, he gets out of his patrol car and walks up to the door and knocks on the door. Mrs. Rodriguez opens the door, and Officer Reid states to her, "Mrs. Rodriguez, if you do not stop calling and harassing Mr. Shelton on the telephone, I will have to arrest you for disturbing the peace." states Officer Reid. "But Officer that is my boy that bastard Mr. Shelton is holding, he has no right!" she screams. Officer Reid raises his hand, "Mrs. Rodriguez, no one is holding your son against his will." replies Officer Reid. "I demand that you return Rhobert home immediately!!" she yells. "Mrs. Rodriguez you are in no position to demand anything. I am taking your son Rhobert to meet with a DCFS Counselor for substantiated child abuse, and if you interfere in any way I will arrest you immediately is that clear?" states Officer Reid. As Officer Reid is leaving to go back to his patrol car dispatch informs him, "Patrol 9, DCFS Counselor Mrs. Sandra MacQuire is waiting for you." Officer Reid replies, "10-4." Officer Reid then returns to Mr. Shelton's house to pick up Rhobert.

Officer Reid then drives Rhobert to the station to meet with the DCFS Counselor. "Rhobert this is Mrs. Sandra MacQuire a DCFS Counselor, she would like to talk with you." states Officer Reid. Officer Reid hands Mrs. MacQuire the cassette recording with the alleged child abuse on it. "Thank you Officer Reid, please let me have some time with Mr. Rodriguez." requests Mrs. MacQuire. "Yes Ma'am, I will be right out side if you need me." replies Officer Reid.

"Rhobert tell me why you are here?" asks Mrs. MacQuire. "Yes Ma'am, my stepmother spanked me with a sweeper cord." replies Rhobert. "Oh my, and why did she do that Rhobert?" asks Mrs. MacQuire. "Because that is what she always does to me. She always beats me with a sweeper cord; this time she beat me with the sweeper cord giving me two hundred and fifty lashes." states Rhobert. "So tell me Rhobert, what did you do that made her want to spank you?" asks Mrs. MacQuire. "I did not do anything. Her son fell down and blamed it on me. He told my stepmother that I pushed him and I did not push him. She believed him and thought that I was lying." states Rhobert. "You said she always spanks you this way. What do you mean by that?" asks Mrs. MacQuire. "She is a mean and evil person. She would always spank me with the sweeper cord for any reason. Every time she spanked me I would have to pull my clothes down and lift my shirt up, grab my ankles, and if I let go she would add more lashes onto the total number of lashes I was to get," states Rhobert. "Did she ever spank her children too?" asks Mrs. MacQuire. "Yes, she would swat their bottom with her hand, with their clothes on," states Rhobert. "So she never spanked her children with the sweeper cord, like the way she did you?" asks Mrs. MacQuire. "No. She never spanked her kids with the sweeper cord. Her children were too good for that type of punishment." replies Rhobert. "So tell me Rhobert, why you didn't ever tell anyone what she was doing to you with the sweeper cord. Why haven't you ever come to me to tell me, before now?" asks Mrs. MacQuire. "Because my stepmother used to work for an attorney and she would tell me that I can go and tell the police or DCFS if I want to. It is just a matter of my word against her word, and they would believe her before they would believe me. Also, they can only by law hold me no more then 48 hours. At which time they would have to return me home to her. When I got home I would get the worst spanking of my life. On several occasions I went to other family and told them. They would call her and talk to her about it. She would tell them some story that they would believe to make them think I was lying and making it up. They would believe her and not me. They would believe that I did something to deserve a spanking. So when I got home, she would spank me even worst just for telling. So I quit telling, and started believing that there was no where I could go to get help." states Rhobert.

"Rhobert can you tell me what is this tape that Officer Reid gave me?" asks Mrs. MacQuire. "Before I left my bedroom to get a spanking, I put a cassette in my tape recorder and pressed record." replies Rhobert. "Why did you do that, what made you think to do that?" asks Mrs. MacQuire. "Well my stepmother always told me no one would believe me that they would only believe her. So I thought that one day I would need this tape to prove her wrong." replies Rhobert. "May I listen to your tape Rhobert?" asks Mrs. MacQuire. "Yes." says Rhobert. Mrs. MacQuire places the cassette into a cassette recorder and begins to listen to it. After a few minutes, with tears in her eyes from the screams of mercy and begging his stepmother to stop, she turns it off. "Don't you want to hear the end?" asks Rhobert. "No son, I've heard enough." States teary eyed Mrs. MacQuire. "Don't you believe me?" asks Rhobert. After a few more tears, and a long pause, Mrs. MacQuire says, "Rhobert, I am so very sorry. No child should ever have to do what you done. No child should ever have to go through what your stepmother has put you through. Yes, your stepmother was right about being required to return you home in 48 hours." Rhobert immediately got scared and began to cry. Mrs. MacQuire continues on, "But Rhobert, that is only if there is no proof or no grounds for holding you. Rhobert you are very strong and courageous for coming to me with this. You have done the right thing. You have given me the proof I need to help you so that your stepmother will never touch you again. And Rhobert, I am so very sorry that you had to endure what you have gone through for so long without any help. Rhobert just so you know, this is going to go to trial before a Judge. I will place you in the Belle Haut Children's Home until the trial. And Rhobert, no Judge on earth will send you back to your stepmother after listening to this tape. OK Rhobert." "Yes Ma'am, and thank you Ma'am." replies Rhobert.

Mrs. MacQuire gets up and opens the door to call Officer Reid into the room, "Officer Reid, I am authorizing Rhobert to be admitted to the Pays des, Illinois Belle Haute Children's Home under their care and custody to await trial. Can you please escort us to the Children's Home?" asks Mrs. MacQuire. "Yes Ma'am, will you both please come with me." states Officer Reid.

Chapter Two

Officer Reid's patrol car and Mrs. MacQuire's DCFS vehicle pull into the parking lot of the Belle Haute Children's Home. The setting sun was over shadowed by the gloomy looking Children's Home. From Rhobert's vantage point the Children's Home looked more like a prison than a home. The dark red brick structure giving way to the black shutters and rusted black barred windows gives Rhobert a very eerie feeling just from the looks of the place.

Officer Reid, Mrs. MacQuire, and Rhobert walk toward the front door of the Children's Home, with Officer Reid in the lead. Mrs. MacQuire signals to Rhobert to wait while Officer Reid walks into the alcove to press the talk button on the speaker box located by the locked door. Rhobert briefly takes a look around noticing that there are no outside cameras trained on the door. A startling voice barks from the speaker box, "Yes, may I help you?" Officer Reid presses the talk button to reply, "Yes, this is Officer

Reid and Mrs. MacQuire from DCFS we have Rhobert Rodriguez with us to be admitted." "OK, I will be right there." the voice from the box replies.

The door to the Children's Home suddenly opens and a tall slender man with a dark beard sticks his hand out to Officer Reid, "Officer Reid, Mrs. MacQuire my name is Mr. William MacKenley. I am the Assistant Administrator of Belle Haute Children's Home. The Administrator, Mr. Bud Dyer is not in tonight. Please, come in and follow me to my office. This way please." states Mr. MacKenley as he locks the door behind them. They all walk through the door into a dark hallway. A light shining from an office gives light to where Mr. MacKenly is leading them. There is a wooden bench outside the office across the hall. "Rhobert please have a seat on the bench for a minute while Officer Reid and I have a talk with Mr. MacKenley. I will come get you." states Mrs. MacQuire. Rhobert takes a seat on the bench watching as Officer Reid and Mrs. MacQuire begin to follow Mr. MacKenley into his office. Then Rhobert turns his gaze towards the quiet dark hallway.

Rhobert's gaze is suddenly broken by a small hardly audible voice of a girl crying out, "No! No! Stop! Please stop! No!" Rhobert looks around to try to make out where the voice is coming from. It sounds like its coming from under the bench. "Please stop! You are hurting me! No!" the voice continues. Rhobert looks down and notices a heater duct next to the bench. He also notices that the begging cries for mercy are coming from heater duct.

Rhobert leans down to get closer to the heater duct, wondering where the audible sounds are coming from. He hears the girl's pleading cries coming from the heater duct. "No! Stop! It hurts! Please, No!." Then suddenly a audible thud comes from the heater duct, and the crying begging voice goes quiet.

"Mr. MacKenley, based on substantial proof of abuse at the child's home, I am removing Rhobert from his home and placing him here in the Belle Haute Children's Home under your protective care. He will remain here as a temporary ward of the state until his trial. Mr. MacKenley, I am warning you, let no harm fall upon Rhobert. Also, let no one, absolutely no one including his family come near him. If any harm comes to Rhobert while he is here waiting for his trial date; I will hold you personally responsible. Is that clear Mr. MacKenley?" "Oh come on Sandra why are you being so hard on me I don't need this." states Mr. MacKenley. "Excuse me, Mr. MacKenley it is Mrs. MacQuire to you. You know, as well as I know that I cannot act on rumors. Mr. MacKenley the rumors of abuse have been flying. Oh, have they been flying. God, how I would love for you to give me just one opportunity to act on something other than a rumor so that I can shut this place down for good! Do you understand me Mr. MacKenley?" angrily asks Mrs. MacQuire. "Yes, Mrs. MacQuire crystal clear. Now if you are done, get the hell out of my Children's Home. I have work to do here!" demands Mr. MacKenley. Mrs. MacQuire goes to the office door and calls Rhobert into the office. Rhobert comes into the office and Mrs. MacQuire takes him over to Mr. MacKenley. "Rhobert, this is Mr. MacKenley the Assistant Administrator of the Belle Haute Children's Home. He will take care of you while you are here." states Mrs. MacQuire. Mr. MacKenley extends his hand out to Rhobert. Rhobert hesitantly puts his hand out to shake hands with Mr. MacKenley as he says, "Hello Rhobert, as Mrs. MacQuire stated I am Mr. MacKenley the Assistant Administrator of the Children's Home. I would like to welcome you to the Belle Haute Children's Home. I will call the House Father to assign you to your bed. Don't worry Rhobert, House Father is merely just the title given to the person in charge of the Boy's Dormitory here at the Children's Home. The House Father will be right with you."

Mr. MacKenley goes to the phone on his desk and calls for the House Father to come receive Rhobert. Mr. MacKenley then turns toward Mrs. MacQuire and says, "Mrs. MacQuire, as soon as you and Officer Reid are ready to leave, I will kindly let you both out. Sorry for the inconvenience, but the Home's entire exit doors are locked from the outside and the inside. Just let me know when you are ready please?" "We are both ready now, thank you." replies Mrs. MacQuire. Mr. MacKenley tells Rhobert, "Rhobert, please wait right here I will be right back."

Mrs. MacQuire and Officer Reid begin to walk towards the door. Mrs. MacQuire turns to tell Rhobert, "I will see you soon Rhobert. You take care alright?" "Thank you." replies Rhobert as they wave good bye. Rhobert's wave good bye was a slow sad wave because he did not want them to go. Mr. MacKenley walks Mrs. MacQuire and Officer Reid to the exit door, and takes out his key to unlock the door to let them out. They leave with the door closing behind them. He locks the door after they leave. Mr. MacKenley returns to his office where Rhobert is waiting for the House Father to come.

With Officer Reid and Mrs. MacQuire now gone, Rhobert turns to face Mr. MacKenley and asks, "Sir, can I tell you something?" "Why sure you can Rhobert." replies Mr. MacKenley. "Well sir, while I was outside the office setting on the bench waiting for Mrs. MacQuire to come get me I heard the voice of a girl crying coming from the heater duct next to the bench." states Rhobert. "Well Rhobert you really have been through a lot of sudden shocking traumatic events of abuse in your life these past few hours. I am sure that it was just your mind playing tricks on you." replies Mr. MacKenley. "Oh no sir, what I heard was real honest." says Rhobert. "Well Rhobert I am sure it was nothing, but I will look into it Rhobert, OK." replies Mr. MacKenley. "OK, thank you sir." says Rhobert as he sits down to wait for the House Father.

The phone on Mr. MacKenley's desk begins to ring and he answers it, "Hello." Unknown to Rhobert it is the House Mother calling Mr. MacKenley. Rhobert can only hear what Mr. MacKenley is saying and Mr. MacKenley knows this too. "Yes sir, it's me Colina the House Mother. I am calling to let you know that Sarah

Dyer is missing, and I don't know where she is." says the House Mother Mrs. Colina Gaven. "Yes of course dear I know." replies Mr. MacKenley, "Mrs. MacQuire from DCFS was here and she just left the both of them." "Oh OK, I did not know that. Thank you Mr. MacKenly, now I can quit worrying. Sorry to have bothered you." says Colina. "No bother at all, thank you Mrs. Gaven. Good job, and thank you for letting me know." says Mr. MacKenley as he hangs up the phone. Rhobert believes that Mr. MacKenley was talking about Mrs. MacQuire and Officer Reid leaving. Rhobert has no idea what that conversation was all about.

Mr. Adair Anderson a strong bulky bald headed man arrives at Mr. MacKenley's office. "Yes Mr. Anderson please come in. Rhobert this is the House Father Mr. Anderson and you will be assigned to him he will take you to your assigned bed now." says Mr. MacKenley. Rhobert gets up and walks over to Mr. Anderson, and Mr. MacKenley tells Mr. Anderson as they start to walk toward the office door, "Mr. Anderson, Rhobert is an NT he has trial coming up." Mr. Anderson gives Mr. MacKenley a thumbs up signal as he and Rhobert walk out the door together. NT is a code word known only by the Children's Home staff and it stands for "No Touch" meaning no whipping, beating, hitting, or biting.

As Rhobert and Mr. Anderson make their way down the long dark hallway, Rhobert notices that there is a lighted adjoining hallway near the far end of the hallway. With his gaze still fixed on the far end of the hallway, Rhobert sees a man in fatigues carrying a shovel hurriedly crossing the lit hallway. Just before they reach the adjoining hallway, Mr. Anderson grabs Rhobert and pins him to the wall with his forearm stretched across his throat making it difficult for Rhobert to breath. Rhobert is shaken and stunned with a terrified look on his face by the unprovoked actions of Mr. Anderson. "Look here you stupid miserable piece of meat, let's get something straight." states Mr. Anderson. "But why are you doing this to me? I did not do anything wrong," asks Rhobert. Pressing and holding Rhobert to the wall with one hand, he smacks Rhobert upside the head with the other, "**SHUT UP! DO NOT INTERUPT ME WHEN I AM TALKING TO YOU! DO YOU UNDERSTAND ME!**" asks Mr. Anderson, not really looking for an answer. "Yes." gasps Rhobert. While still holding Rhobert to the wall with one hand, Mr. Anderson smacks Rhobert upside the head again. "**YOU WILL ADDRESS ME AS SIR WHEN TALKING TO ME! DO I MAKE MYSELF CLEAR?**" loudly screams Mr. Anderson. Very scared and shaken Rhobert gasps, "Yes sir." Mr. Anderson grabs Rhobert and pushes him down the hall. Stumbling Rhobert is able regain his balance to keep from falling. Mr. Anderson pushes him from behind to hurry him along causing him to stumble again. Rhobert is able to keep his balance to keep from falling as they make their way into the Boy's Dormitory. Mr. Anderson grabs a thin cane pole by the door as they walk into the Boy's Dormitory.

Mr. Anderson pushes Rhobert up against an empty

bed, "Take off all of your clothes and put on the shirt and pants that are on your bed." angrily states Mr. Anderson. The shirt and pants that are lying on the unmade bed are similar to hospital gowns. Rhobert hurriedly gets dressed, Mr. Anderson smacks the unmade bed with his cane pole, "On your bed you will find a pillow case, a mattress cover, and a sheet. Make your bed and do it now." orders Mr. Anderson. "Yes sir." replies Rhobert as he begins to make his bed. Once Rhobert is finished making his bed he looks to Mr. Anderson who walks up to Rhobert standing by the side of his bed. Mr. Anderson reaches down and pulls the mattress cover and sheet off the made bed and throws them on the floor telling Rhobert with the cane pole sticking in his chest, "**I TOLD YOU TO MAKE YOUR BED!**" "Yes sir." replies Rhobert as he picks up the mattress cover and bed sheet from off the floor. As Rhobert hurriedly makes his bed again, one of the boys next to his bed turns over to look at what is going on in the room with Rhobert and Mr. Anderson. Mr. Anderson brutally strikes the boy with his cane pole several times yelling, "**THIS DOES NOT CONCERN YOU! ROLL OVER AND MIND YOUR OWN BUSINESS!**" Tears and cries of agony can be heard coming from the boy as he rolls over in his bed. Turning his attention back to Rhobert and the made bed, Mr. Anderson reaches for the pillow shaking it so the pillow falls to the floor leaving the pillow case in his hand. Mr. Anderson throws the pillow case across the floor and tells Rhobert, "**I SAID MAKE YOUR BED MISTER.**" Mr. Anderson smacks Rhobert across the legs with his cane pole. Rhobert clinches his teeth from the agonizing pain as tears begin to swell in his eyes. Rhobert hurries across the room to get his pillow case and returns to his bed to pick up the pillow lying on the floor. He puts the pillow back into the pillow case and places it back on the bed. When suddenly the phone on the wall by the door begins to ring, Mr. Anderson stops his brutal torment and walks over to the phone to answer it. "Hello Anderson here." states Mr. Anderson on the phone. "Yes sir, be right there." replies Mr. Anderson. Mr. Anderson turned toward Rhobert before leaving and says to him, "You wait till I get back." Then he rushes out the door. With Mr. Anderson gone, the room gets quiet except for a few muffled moans and groans from the boy by Rhobert's bed that had been beaten by Mr. Anderson with his cane pole.

Angry and upset Rhobert hurriedly puts his street clothes back on that were placed on the empty bed next to his bed. He walks over to the door and looks down the long hallway and he sees no one. Then he looks the other way towards the exit door and does not see anyone by the exit door. He walks out into the hallway and sneaks over to the exit door, pushes on the bar to open the door. The door quietly opens Rhobert rushes outside with the door closing behind him. Rhobert rushes out a few yards and comes to an immediate stop looking around. A sudden feeling of sadness overcomes Rhobert as he discovers that he is in the backyard of the Children's Home. The backyard is completely surrounded by a twelve foot high brick wall with rolled barbed wire on the top of the wall. The brick wall starts from one end of the Children's Home, and loops around the backyard to the other end of the Children's Home; with no opening for entry or exit. There is but one tree in the middle of the backyard and that tree is nowhere near the brick wall either. Let alone the barbed wire on top of the brick wall that he would need to get over as well. Rhobert realizes that there is no need to try to climb the tree to get over the high brick wall, since the tree and its branches are nowhere near the brick wall. He also knows that he is way too small to try to climb the brick wall himself. Rhobert sulks miserably back to the exit door in the alcove that he just came out of to try to get back in. He is not surprised to learn that the exit door is locked on the outside. Rhobert sees a talk box by the door with the talk button on it. He cannot bring himself to press the talk button, because he knows doing so would definitely mean trouble for him. Rhobert remembers what Mr. MacKenley had told Mrs. MacQuire, that all of the exit doors to the Children's Home are locked on the inside and out. He realizes that there is no need to lock the door on the inside, since no one could exit the backyard anyway. Rhobert sits down by the locked door putting his hands on his head resting his head on his knees and begins to cry.

CHAPTER THREE

The Mr. Anderson slows his hurried walk to an arrogant stop at the doorway to Mr. MacKenley's Office. He props himself up in the doorway and raps on the door a couple times. "Oh yes Adair, please come on in." says Bill. "Care to join me for a drink?" asks Bill. "Sure, I'd love one." says Adair. Bill goes over to the credenza while Adair sits down making himself comfortable. Bill takes down two large shot glasses then grabs an antique flask and pours the two shot glasses. Bill hands a shot glass to Adair, who takes a sip. "Wow what is this stuff Bill, this is really good?" asks Adair. "Well Adair this is my vintage original Scottish Highland liqueur which is named Bruadar. It is Scottish Gaelic for - a dream." states Bill. "A friend of mine told me about this liqueur when I hired our cook Mrs. Dulcie Hayes. My friend recommended to me that I hire her. She comes from a Welch background. Thought I would give this liqueur my friend told me about a try." says Bill as he holds his shot glass up looking at it before taking a sip. "How is she working out Bill?" asks Adair. "She's working out really well Adair. She loves her job, and I have not heard any bad words about her. She is a really good cook too." replies Bill. They both continue to sip their liqueur.

"So Adair did you get Rhobert settled in?" asks Bill. "Yea, it is all new to him, he will learn soon enough though. I did have trouble with one of the boys that is bunked next him, but I quickly took care of that." replies Adair. "Well good Adair. Oh hey Adair, just to let you know Colina called me this evening to tell me that Sarah Dyer was missing. Seems Mr. Torey Reid our Maintenance Grounds Technician was at it again." says Bill. "Yea, I was wondering. I saw Torey in the hallway leaving in a hurry with a shovel in his hand." replies Adair. "Well Rhobert heard it all as it was happening Adair." says Bill. "Oh really, how could he I wonder, he wasn't there was he?" asks Adair. "Well no of course not. Rhobert told me he heard everything going on coming from the heater duct by the bench. He heard everything including her begging for her life before she was silenced." says Bill. "I take it this all occurred in solitary? Torey must have taken her there. That is the only place sounds from the heater duct by bench could be heard from." asks Adair. "Well yes Adair that is true, and keep in mind that if they could be heard from the bench in the hallway; then they can also be heard in the Administrator's Office too. Damned good thing Bud was out tonight." says Bill. "Well Bill I have an idea on how we could reduce noise coming from solitary." states Adair. "OK Adair I am listening." replies Bill. "Well Bill we can put squares of fiberglass insulation the size of the heater duct with rubber squares as baffles in between the fiberglass insulation squares in the heater duct in solitary, and also in the heater duct in the hallway. I can take care of that tomorrow, and when I am done, we can test it out to see if that works." states Adair. "Wow Adair that sounds like it might work. OK Adair good idea let's give it a try. Let me know when you got it done, and Adair do not tell anyone about this but me. If anyone asks you what you are doing refer them to me, let me take care of it." states Bill. "Yes sir I understand." replies Adair. "Also Adair while you are down in solitary if you don't mind check out behind the cellar door for me make sure everything is OK there, and make sure Torey cleaned his mess up too." asks Bill. "Yes Bill, will do, and yes Bill I will only tell you." replies Adair. Adair sets his empty shot glass down on Bill's desk and stands up to leave. "Adair do be very careful in that cellar, it is a dead zone. There is over 40 years of death in that room." states Bill. "I understand Bill." replies Adair as he walks out of Bill's office.

The telephone in the Maintenance Garage begins to ring. Torey Reid answers it, "Maintenance." "She was good wasn't she? Did you enjoy it? Now be a good boy and do him now too, or you are going to be next. See that box wrapped up on your table, go ahead open it up?" says the voice on the phone. Torey opens the box on the table, and then opens the box that was wrapped. He sees two real human eye balls looking at him. He immediately sets the box down screaming, "Oh God! Oh God!" Still on the phone the voice tells Torey, "Now remember I am watching you the eye's are upon you. Do what I say or die." a voice begins laughing and then hangs up. Torey yells, "Who is this?" as the line goes dead. Torey slams the receiver down screaming, "Damn it, shit."

Adair walks down the hallway to a locked door with a misleading label that reads, "STORAGE ONLY NOT AN EXIT." Using his key he unlocks and opens the door that leads to the solitary confinement. He steps through the door onto the steps that lead to solitary in the basement. The door closes behind him. Adair pauses for a moment and looks down the dark stairwell into total gloomy darkness. He then reaches over and flips the switch to turn on the lights to the stairwell and solitary. The lights come on and immediately brighten up the cement block stairwell and the cement block solitary room. Adair slowly proceeds step by step down the stairwell looking very closely at the cement walls and the cement steps checking for any sign of dirt, stains, or blood. Not finding anything he continues down one step at a time. After a long thorough check of each step of the stairwell Adair finally makes it to the cement floor of solitary. The cement stairwell wall on the right continues along the southern end of solitary. There are two doors on the southern wall. One off the stairwell and it is a closet door. The other door in the middle of this southern wall is a small wooden door which makes up the access into the cellar crawl space behind the door. This wooden cellar access door is six inches above the cement floor and is three feet wide by four feet high. The wall on the left proceeds out for about seven feet and it is only five feet high leaving four feet of open space from the top of the wall to the ceiling of solitary. This wall stops before the passageway which runs down the middle of solitary towards the northern wall of solitary. The passageway is only five feet wide, on the other side of the passageway there is another wall five feet high. This wall runs another seven feet before connecting to the eastern wall of solitary. Adair slowly walks along each wall in the space besides the southern wall. There is a six inch hole in the cement floor of the space before the small wooden cellar door. He stops before the small wooden cellar door on the southern wall. Looking down he finds a lot of dirt on the cement floor beneath the small wooden cellar door, and on the lip directly under the cellar door. He reaches into his pocket to get the key to the cellar door, and he opens the cellar door. As he opens the small cellar door, a little more dirt falls onto the lip of the doorway and onto the cement floor. A very strong foul odor comes from the cellar from years of death and rotting corpses. As he holds his breath, he looks through the door opening into the dirty crawl space. Looking into the crawl space there is what appears to be a trench dug into the dirt that is as wide as the door and level with the bottom of the doorway which proceeds to the far end of the crawl space. The dirt side walls of the trench rise up about a foot and a half before leveling out on each side of the doorway to the cellar. Adair looks into the crawl space and follows the trench to the far end of the crawl space and notices a small steel door with large handles and hinges on it. It looks to be like an old coal burning furnace. He did not notice any disturbance in the length of the trench. He then looks to the right of the trench where the dirt has leveled out and does not notice any kind of disturbance. He looks to the left of the trench where the dirt has leveled out and notices the dirty bloody body of a half buried little girl. Still holding his breath he bends down to crawl into the crawl space. He then leans over the left side of the trench to open the dirty bloody jaw of the little girl. With her jaw open he looks into her mouth and notices that all of her teeth have been pulled from her mouth. He then crawls backwards and out of the crawl space access and stands straight up. He covers his nose with his dirty hand and takes a quick breath while grabbing and shutting the small cellar access door. He begins to breathe normally, gets the key to the cellar access door and locks the door. He then wipes off his clothes with his hands knocking off all the loose dirt from his clothes onto the cement floor.

Adair then turns to face the northern wall of solitary and looks down the aisle in the middle of solitary. On each side of the aisle there are six cubicles. The western wall of solitary makes up the back wall to the six cubicles on the left. The eastern wall of solitary makes up the back wall to the six cubicles on the right. Five foot high seven foot long cement walls make up the side walls to each cubicle and each of these walls are connected to the back wall of the side they are on. Except for the last cubicles on the left and right side at the far end of the aisle, the northern wall makes up one of the side walls to those two cubicles. In the center of the aisle and across from the cubicles on the left and right, there is a six inch hole in the cement floor of the aisle. Three inches below the level of the cement floor in each hole is a grated metal drain. Looking down the aisle there is six cubicles on each side and six holes in the cement floor in the center of the aisle. Adair walks down the aisle and stops at the first two cubicles, one on the left and one on the right. In each cubicle there are two half round steel bars protruding from the back wall, and also two half round steel bars protruding from the cement floor of each cubicle. Each steel bar is one half inch in diameter. Attached to each bar in the cubicles is a three foot chain, and at the end of each chain is a locking shackle. The bars and chains in each cubicle have long since become rusted over the years. He looks into the cubicle on the left and then the one on the right and notices nothing out of the ordinary. Checking each wall and cement floor of each cubicle. He then looks into the drain in the cement floor for these two cubicles and notices a slight stain of blood on the drain. The slight stain of blood in the drain leads Adair to believe that the girl died in one of these two cubicles the one on the left or the one on the right. He gives the cubicle on the right a more detailed look and finds nothing. He gives the cubicle on the left a more detailed look and he finds a few long strands of dark long hair tangled up in one of the chains.

He completely removes all of the pieces of hair found. The color of the hair matches the color of the hair found on the little girl buried in the cellar. Adair now believes he knows which cubicle that the little girl died in. Adair continues up the aisle checking out the remaining cubicles and the remaining drains finding nothing.

Finished checking, Adair goes to the closet door on the southern wall and opens the door. Inside the closet is a rolled up garden water hose with spray nozzle on one end, and the other end is connected to a faucet on the wall inside the closet. Adair reaches up on the shelf in the closet and grabs two bottles of bleach and a bristle broom from the closet. He pours bleach on the entire cement floor through out solitary and in all of the cubicles. He then scrubs the cement floor through out solitary and all of the cubicles. He puts the empty bleach containers in a trash can in the closet and grabs the spray nozzle of the water hose turning on the water to the water hose. He walks out of the closet dragging the water hose with him and fully opens the spray nozzle spraying the cement floor of solitary and all of the cubicles. Adair returns the water hose to the closet rolling it back up. Wearing rubber gloves Adair then goes and thoroughly cleans with bleach the drain that he found the blood stain in. Adair goes back to the closet and gets the caulking gun. He then goes to the cellar access door and seals it with the caulk in order to seal in the very strong decades of decay odor. He then returns to the closet to put away the caulk gun, and grabs the large spray bottle of Industrial Strength Odor

Eliminator. He sprays the entire solitary before returning the bottle to the closet.

Satisfied that solitary is forensically cleaned to his standards, Adair goes up the steps to leave solitary turning off the lights at the top of the stairwell. He hurries down the hall to the Assistant Administrator's office to see if Bill is still there. The light of Bill's office down the hall suddenly goes out Adair see's Bill leaving in the hallway and calls out to him, "Bill, it's me Adair." "Yes Adair, I was just leaving what do you need?" asks Bill. "Well Bill I wanted to let you know that I checked out the cellar and it is OK. I also cleaned the entire solitary I found a blood stain, hair, and dirt it really needed to be cleaned up. Tomorrow I will work on the heater ducts." replies Adair. "Good job Adair, go check on your kids now. I will see you in the morning." states Bill. "Thank you, have a good night Bill." replies Adair. "You too." says Bill as he heads for the exit door. Adair watches as Bill takes out his key to unlock the exit door to leave.

Pleased that Bill approves of his good job cleaning solitary, Adair walks down the hall back to the Boy's Dormitory to check on Rhobert. As he is walking down the hall Adair remembers that he did not collect Rhobert's clothes. He reminds himself to do that when he gets to the Boy's Dormitory. As he walks into the Boy's Dormitory looking down, he grabs his cane pole that is leaning against the wall by the door. He takes a few steps into the dormitory and comes to a complete stop, frozen in his steps. Shocked and perplexed by what he sees in the dormitory his mouth falls open with nothing to say; and he did not want to awaken the other boys with any sudden loud noises. His wide eyed gaze fixed on the boy he had told to turn over and beaten with his cane pole was swinging lifeless above his bed from a bed sheet that he used to hang himself with. Momentarily breaking his gaze off the swinging boy, Adair looks and is even more stunned to discover that Rhobert is not in his bed and his street clothes are gone. Perplexed with these sudden events unfolding before him looks at the swinging boy, then at Rhobert's empty bed, back to the swinging boy, and then back at Rhobert's empty bed. His mind is momentarily confused; he thinks to himself, *Oh God! What do I do now? Do I run searching the Children's Home looking for Rhobert, or do I take care of this swinging boy? What do I do with this swinging boy?* He clinches his teeth, squeezes and makes a strong fist with his right hand, and begins pounding with all his might his right fist into his left hand mumbling, "Damn! Damn! Damn!"

CHAPTER FOUR

The exit door that Rhobert is sitting by is recessed in an alcove of the Children's Home. Tired and half awake Rhobert leans against the wall in the alcove. Still unable to muster up the courage to press the talk button on the speaker box by the door and announce his missing presence. Suddenly Rhobert hears another door opening. Since it is not the door that he is sitting by, he peaks around the alcove and watches a girl coming out of the only another alcove along the exterior wall of the Children's Home. Watching the girl he thinks to himself that must be the exit to the backyard from the Girl's Dormitory. The girl is constantly looking over her shoulder to make sure that she is not being watched or followed as she makes her way to the tree in the middle of the yard. When she gets to the tree she kneels down by the tree, makes a sign of the cross, folding her hands to pray. Rhobert gets up and quietly moves out of the alcove going out towards the girl by the tree. As Rhobert gets close to the girl she hears him approaching and she looks over her shoulder to find Rhobert there, terrified she cries out and runs behind the tree. "Stay away do not touch me, please! I did not do anything wrong! I was just coming out here to pray; please, I will go back in! I am sorry, I should have stayed inside! Leave me alone, please!" she cries out. Rhobert stops and stands still, "OK, OK, wait. I only just want to talk to you." "No you do not. You are one of them. You want to kill me too!" she cries. "No, I do not want to kill you. I just want to talk to you." says Rhobert. "You are lying! Just stay away I do not know you! Please, just leave me alone!" she cries. "Look I do not know you either. My name is Rhobert Rodriguez. I am new here the police and DCFS just brought me here. I was trying to run away from this place. I ran outside because the door was not locked, and when I did it locked me out here. I thought I was free until I got out here and saw these high walls with barbed wire on top of them. Now I am stuck out here. I know if I try to use the talk box to get back in then they will know I tried to run away and they will beat me again. I dare not try to use that speaker box by the door, and then they will know. I was so very happy to see you come out here when you did. I notice that you used something to block the door from closing and locking on you so that you can get back in. Why are you out here anyway? You obviously do not want to run away." asks Rhobert. "I am out here because nine months ago they killed my sister after she tried to run away and they buried her under this tree along with the woman whose house she ran away too,"

34

says the girl. "Oh my God I am so very sorry for you." says Rhobert. "I sneak out here after everyone is asleep to visit and pray for my sister. You should not run away Rhobert they would kill you too." says the girl. "How do you know all this, I am sorry what is your name?" asks Rhobert. "My name is Carla." says Carla Ashton. "OK, Carla how do you know so much about them killing?" asks Rhobert. "Because that is what they do Rhobert. They kill for fun, and they kill those who try to tell on them. They killed my sister. She ran away to a woman's house and told the woman what was going on here. The woman came to the Children's Home with the police to turn them in. They killed the woman and buried her by this tree. Then they went to the woman's home and found my sister there. They killed my sister and buried her by the tree too." replies Carla. Rhobert asks Carla, "How do you know they killed your sister Carla?" "I watched them bury both of them out here, and then I heard them talking about it later." replies Carla. "Oh my God Carla, I am so very sorry that happened." responds Rhobert. "Every time someone comes up missing here it is because they probably killed them too." says Carla. "How many boys and girls have come up missing since you have been here, besides your sister?" asks Rhobert. "I do not know about the boys, but since I have been here fifteen girls have supposedly left." replies Carla. "So you do not know if the ones that have left were killed or not?" asks Rhobert. "No, I do not know since we are not allowed to communicate with the outside world." replies Carla. "Do your parents know about what they did to your sister?" asks Rhobert. "My parents are dead. They died in a car crash. That is why my sister and I were brought here." replies Carla choking back a few tears. "Oh my, I am so very sorry to hear that Carla. I did not know." replies Rhobert. They both got very quiet, and after what seemed like forever to Rhobert, Rhobert speaks up, "Well, I guess I better get back inside before they find me gone." With that Rhobert starts to walk towards the other open door. Rhobert gets a few steps away when Carla quietly calls out to him, "Rhobert wait!" Rhobert stops, begins to turn and Carla runs up to him takes his hand with both of her two hands gently squeezes Rhobert's hand and asks, "Rhobert, will you please be my friend?" Rhobert puts his other hand on hers smiles and softly replies, "Yes Carla I really would love to be your friend." Then Rhobert asks Carla, "Carla, will you be my friend?" She takes a second to wipe her tears away, looks at Rhobert smiling for once as she replies, "Yes Rhobert I really would like to be your friend too." Astonishingly their eyes meet and momentarily they both can see each other's love in their heart's even through all the pain that they both have been through. "I need to get back in." states Rhobert. "Yea me too." says Carla not letting go of Rhobert's hand. They both walk together hand in hand to the cracked open Girl's Dormitory backyard exit door.

As they both enter the alcove, Rhobert positions himself in front of Carla and says, "Let me check to make sure the coast is clear." "OK." replies Carla. Rhobert slightly opens the door and pushes aside with his foot what Carla was using to block the door open, and looks inside. Seeing no movement in the dark hallway, Rhobert quietly goes inside waving for Carla to come in behind him and they both hug the wall moving towards the entrance to the Girl's Dormitory. Rhobert quickly looks into the Girl's Dormitory and goes back to tell Carla the coast is still clear. "Thank you Rhobert. Please be careful." says Carla as she kisses Rhobert on the cheek and quickly goes inside to get into her bed.

Rhobert quickly crosses the hall and hugs the wall moving quickly toward the adjoining hall. Rhobert turns down the long adjoining hall hugging wall. He comes to a door, the label on the door curiously catches his eye, and he then stops to take a look. The door is labeled, "INTERVIEW ROOM 1". Rhobert checks the door and it is unlocked, so he opens the door to peek in. He sees a bare mattress with no sheets or covers. He also notices that all the walls are covered from top to bottom with three inch foam that has cones reset into the foam, apparently for sound proofing the room. After having good look, Rhobert then shuts the door and continues to move along the wall. He then comes to another door that is labeled, "INTERVIEW ROOM 2." This door is also unlocked, so Rhobert peeks into this room. The room is very similar to the previous room. So Rhobert closes the door and continues along the wall. As he approaches the adjoining hall where the Boy's Dormitory is Rhobert hears commotion coming from the Boy's Dormitory and slows down. When Rhobert gets to the edge he quickly peeks around the corner to see what the commotion is all about. Rhobert sees both the House Father and that same man in fatigues struggling to drag a large full duffle bag out the exit door to the backyard where he had just recently come from. Once both of them are outside, Rhobert quickly moves into the Boy's Dormitory to his bed. Rhobert rapidly takes off his street clothes folds them up and sets them on the empty bed next to his. He then puts on the clothes that he was given and gets into his bed under the covers. Rhobert then hears the exit door opening again and a man yelling, "I thought you grabbed the shovels, dang it. Hold on I'll go get them." The man comes inside disappears down the hall, and in a few minutes he comes back carrying two shovels. Rhobert hears the man going out of the exit door, and the exit door closing. Rhobert gets up out of bed and quickly goes to look out window of the exit door to see just what they are doing. In the far right corner of the Children's Home backyard, Rhobert sees the two men digging what appears to be a big hole. Finished watching Rhobert then goes and gets back into his bed and covers up. Unable to fall asleep Rhobert begins to wonder just what is going on outside in the backyard. Why does a hole need to be dug in the backyard this late at night, and what does the big duffle bag have to do with digging a big hole? Then all of a sudden Rhobert realizes that he should be very thankful for coming inside from the backyard when he was outside with Carla. Things could have got pretty ugly had the two of them got caught outside. Slowly Rhobert starts to drift off to sleep.

While Adair and Torey are busy digging a two foot wide, five foot long, and six feet deep hole in the backyard of the Children's Home, Torey asks Adair, "I wonder what made this little shit want to hang himself?" "I do not know for sure Torey, and I really do not care right now. The little bastard could have picked a better time to off himself. I have not been able to take a nap or sleep all day and all night. I have been so damned busy." replies Adair. "Yea me too, I know how you feel." says Torey. After a few more minutes of digging Torey stops and says, "OK man there we go the hole is ready for this one." Adair reaches into his back pocket for the pliers and a zip-lock bag and says, "Alright let me get the teeth." "I have always wondered about that Adair. Why do we always have to get their teeth?" asks Torey. Adair unzips the duffle bag then he opens the boy's jaw pulling out all of the teeth with the pliers and puts them in the zip-lock bag. "All I know is, it helps to prevent identification later on." replies Adair. After Adair is done pulling the teeth they both then roll the body into the big hole. They both begin filling the dirt back into the hole over the lifeless body. Once they have finished filling the dirt back into the hole Adair sets his shovel down and tells Torey, "Take care of the rest Torey, I am going to go back inside." "OK Adair I sure will." replies Torey.

Adair goes back through the exit door using his keys, and then proceeds into the Boy's Dormitory. He is very surprised to see Rhobert sleeping in his bed, and his street clothes folded up setting on the opposite bed. Adair shakes his head wondering just where Rhobert had gone to. Although he is glad that Rhobert was gone and did not witness the hanging. Adair grabs Rhobert's street clothes and takes them to his office that is in the back of the dorm. Tired Adair then lies down on the bed in his office to rest.

Mrs. Dulcie Hayes arrives at the Belle Haute Children's Home and parks her car in the parking lot. She gets out of her car, locks the door, straightens her slacks, and begins to walk the sidewalk to the front door in the alcove. On her way up to the front door, she sees Mr. Torey Reid busy on his knee's arranging a tarp in the flower beds that are in front of the evergreen bushes which lines the front of the Children's Home. Torey looks up and see's Mrs. Hayes approaching and says, "Hello Mrs. Hayes, your early today." "Hello Mr. Reid, yes I'm early. Mr. MacKenley asked me to come in and get the children's breakfast started early because Senator MacKenzie is coming to visit today." replies Mrs. Hayes. "Oh yea that is right, I almost forgot. Thank you Mrs. Hayes, and have a good day." says Torey. "You too Mr. Reid." replies Mrs. Hayes as she reaches into her purse for the keys to unlock the front door. She unlocks the front door and goes inside. Torey continues his work in the flower beds. Satisfied that his work in the flower beds is done, Torey picks up his shovel and rake places them behind the evergreen bush. Torey then squeezes into the evergreen bush kneels down on the ground on his knee's with a crowbar in hand, and patiently waits.

After a little while, Mr. Bud Dyer the Headmaster arrives at the Belle Haute Children's Home and parks his car in his designated parking spot in the parking lot. He gets out of his car, locks the door, and begins to walk the sidewalk to the front door in the alcove. He gets to the front door in the alcove, reaches into his pocket for the key when suddenly he is struck from behind in the head and collapses. His keys fall to the ground. Quickly, Torey picks up the keys and puts them in his pocket. Torey tosses the crowbar behind the evergreen bush with the rest of his tools, and starts to drag Mr. Dyer's lifeless body over to the green tarp he has staged. Mr. Dyer's body falls into the hole that the green tarp was covering. Torey then hurriedly grabs the shovel and begins to fill the dirt back into the hole. After the hole is filled, Torey quickly replants the flowers into the flower bed, he then goes and picks up the crowbar. With crowbar in hand, Torey then goes to Mr. Dyer's car he unlocks the door gets in. He tosses the crowbar in the back seat, and starts the car up. He pulls the car out and stops by his Maintenance Garage. Leaving the car running he gets out goes into the garage. Coming back with three full gas cans, he sets them down and opens the back door. He then puts the three gas cans on the floor in the back. He picks up a large rock and places it on the back seat shutting the back door. He gets back into the car and drives up the road twenty miles to a scenic drive. Slowing down on the scenic drive he pulls the car over on the other side of the road perpendicular to the road and points the car at the guard rail that is on the other side of the road. With the car in park and running, he gets out of the car opens the back door and takes the lids off of the three gas cans that he had put on the floor board. He then picks up the large rock he brought, closes the back door and opens the driver door. Torey then puts the large rock on the gas pedal and the engine starts to rev up. He rolls the drive door window down. He closes the driver door, and throws his gloves into the car. He lights a match and tosses it in the back, one of the gas containers catches on fire. As the fire begins to rage he quickly reaches in puts the car in drive. The burning car immediately lunges forward, crashes through the guard rail, and the exploding fire ball tumbles down the ravine. The tumbling ball of fire, finally coming to rest on the water below and slowly begins to sink into the depths of the water. Torey then crosses the street, takes the limbs from off his motorcycle he had previously hid there. He starts it up, puts his helmet on, climbs on and rides back to the Children's Home. Arriving back at the Children's Home, Torey picks up his flower bed tools and shovel takes them to put them away. He then comes back to the alcove of the front door looking for signs of blood that needs to be cleaned up. Not finding any, he still cleans the entire area in the alcove with bleach. Pleased that the alcove is clean, he returns to the Maintenance Garage. Tired he lies down on the cot that he has in the garage, and falls fast asleep.

Chapter Five

Mr. Douglas Quinn the Janitor arrives at the Belle Haute Children's Home and parks his car in the parking lot. He gets out of his car, locks the door, and begins to walk the sidewalk to the front door in the alcove as he always does every morning. He locked the doors to his car; because he remembers that when he was hired on he was told to make sure the doors to his vehicle are locked while at the Children's Home in case one of the children escapes and tries to run away. At the alcove to the front door of the Children's Home he takes the keys from his work belt unlocks the door and goes inside, making sure that the door closes behind him he locks the door. He continues up the hallway passing the administration offices and stopping at the door labeled, "CLEANING LOCKER." He unlocks the door and opens it, pulling out his cleaning cart. He grabs a new trash bag liner and arranges it on his cart. He then logs his start time on his time sheet. Shuts and locks the door and pushes his cart back down the hall to the administration offices. He unlocks the Headmaster's Secretary's Office door, turns on the light and begins to clean her office. After cleaning her office he goes into the Headmaster's Office turns on the light and begins to clean his office. Office cleaning normally consisted of dusting, vacuuming, emptying trash cans and putting a new trash can liner in the trash can putting the full trash can liner in the trash bag on the cart; also gathering any dirty kitchen utensils, plates, and drinking glasses to be returned to the kitchen for cleaning. After he is finished cleaning the Headmaster's Office, he turns out the light and leaves the office going back into the Secretary's Office turning out the light, and then he closes and locks the door. He then crosses the hall unlocks the Assistant Headmaster's Office opens the door turns on the light and begins to clean the office. He picks up two dirty shot glasses and places them onto his cart to take to the kitchen. After cleaning that office he then turns out the light, closing and locking the door, and pushes his cart to the kitchen.

Doug enters the large lighted dining area, leaving his cart just inside the door. Picks up the two shot glasses and begins to head for the kitchen area. On his way he see's Mrs. Dulcie Hayes setting up the dining area for breakfast. "Good morning Mrs. Hayes." says Doug. "Good morning Mr. Quinn, the coffee is ready why don't you go ahead and grab yourself of cup." smiling says Dulcie. "Well thank you Ma'am I sure will get me some, just let me set these glasses down." replies Doug. Doug puts the shot glasses in the deep sink and grabs a clean coffee cup and pours himself a cup of coffee. On his way back to his cart he tells Dulcie, "Thanks again Mrs. Hayes. I'd love to stay and talk, but I have got to get back to my cleaning I am only here part time." Doug sets his coffee down on his cart pushing it out into the hall to continue on with his cleaning.

Ms. Christal MacKenley the Headmaster's Secretary arrives at the Belle Haute Children's Home and parks her car in her designated spot in the parking lot. She gets out of her car, locks the door, straightens her dress, and begins to walk the sidewalk to the front door in the alcove. She notices that her boss's car the Headmaster is not here yet. Thinking to herself that he would be here early today because of the important Senator visit. When she finally reaches the alcove she gets her keys to open the front door. She then proceeds to her office unlocks the door to let herself in. Opens the door turns on the light setting her purse down on her desk. Then she goes into the Headmaster's Office turns on the light, walks over to the coffee maker and starts the coffee. She returns to her office sits down at her desk, and then puts her purse into the drawer of her desk. She then turns on her computer. Picks up her phone dials Bud's home phone, gets no answer. So she dials his cell phone, and still no answer. She hangs up her phone thinking to herself that the no answer on both phones was odd; but she disregards the thought knowing he will either show up, or she will try calling again in a few.

Bill arrives at the Belle Haute Children's Home and parks his car in his designated spot in the parking lot. He gets out of his car, locks the door, and begins to walk the sidewalk to the front door in the alcove. He takes notice that Bud has not arrived yet; which is odd due to the pending Senator visit scheduled for today. He knows that Bud would not want to miss this event, and like the others he would want to be early to make sure things at the Children's Home are going well. When he gets to the alcove and takes out his keys to open the front door. He steps inside and locks the door, and he then proceeds to his office unlocking the door to let himself in. Bill opens the door turns on the light and sets down at his desk turning on his computer. He stands up, grabs his coffee cup and walks across the hall to see his sister Christal. He walks in and says, "Good morning sis." "Oh hi Bill, go ahead coffee's ready." she replies. While walking to get some coffee he asks, "Heard from Bud yet?" "No not yet, he's not answering either of his phones, but I will try again in a few." she replies. "OK, let me know if you get through to him please?" asks Bill. "I sure will Bill." replies Christal as Bill walks out of her office with his coffee.

Bill goes back into his office sits down and calls Colina's office, "Yes good morning Colina let's get the kids up, thank you." Hanging up he calls Adair's office, he lets the phone keep ringing until Adair finally answers, "Hey good morning sleepy head, let's get the kids up. OK, see you later."

Waking up, Adair puts Rhobert's street clothes in a

bag, and labels the bag with Rhobert's name. He then places the bag on a shelf in the street clothes cabinet in his office. Adair then walks over to the dormitory door picks up his cane pole turning on all the lights to begin his normal morning ritual. He begins walking up the aisle yelling, "**OK LADIES RISE AND SHINE, TIME TO GET UP!**" When Adair gets to the end of the aisle, he turns around. As he walks back down the aisle hurtfully smacking with his cane pole anyone who is slow to get up. Yelling at them as he does ignoring cries of agony, "**COMMON, I SAID LET'S GET UP!**" "OK boys, let's get in line by the door." orders Adair. Adair walks along the line of boys waiting at the door, and with his cane pole he moves Rhobert out of the line telling him, "No Rhobert, you wait here with me." Adair turns looks to see who is at the head of the line and says, "OK Greg, go ahead and take them to eat." The line starts to move single file out of the door into the hall and toward the kitchen dining room.

Once that the line of boys is gone from the room Adair turns his focus back on Rhobert. "Alright Rhobert I have a surprise for you for that little stunt you pulled last night. Come with me." says Adair as he grabs Rhobert's arm and leads him out of the dorm and down the hall. When Adair gets to the door labeled, "STORAGE ONLY NOT AN EXIT" he stops takes out his keys. He unlocks and opens the door turning on the lights. He then guides Rhobert down the steps into solitary. Once at the bottom of the steps, he places Rhobert by the cellar door, and tells

Rhobert, "Wait right here Rhobert and don't move." He then walks into the cubical aisle to check which cubical to put Rhobert in. He picks one, and readies the chains. While waiting, still standing Rhobert looks around sees the cellar door with the caulking all around it. Rhobert notices that a key is still in the lock of the cellar door; apparently it must have been overlooked, either way Rhobert quickly reaches out takes the key and puts it in his pocket. Finished Adair returns and grabs Rhobert pushing him into the cubical aisle stopping at the cubical he has picked out for Rhobert. Adair tells Rhobert, "OK Rhobert strip, put your clothes that you were issued on these hooks." He points to the hooks that are near the top of the cubical wall. The only clothes that the children in the Children's Home are issued is like the hospital gowns, a top and a pair of pants, no underwear. Rhobert embarrassingly takes off his clothes and hangs them on one of the hooks. Adair pushes Rhobert into the middle of the cubical up against the back wall and tells Rhobert, "Sit down." Adair then begins to lock the shackles that are on the end of each chain onto Rhobert's wrists and ankles, a total of four one for each wrist and one for each ankle. Pleased that Rhobert is now properly shackled, he steps out of the cubical. "Sir, what if I need to go to the bathroom?" asks Rhobert. "That is what is so neat about solitary Rhobert, just pick a spot and go." laughingly replies Adair. "This will maybe help you to never want to pull another stunt like that again. Oh yea I almost forgot, like Motel Six, we leave the lights on for you." laughingly continues Adair as he walks away. Rhobert hears Adair walking up the steps, the door opening, and closing. He does not hear the door being locked, so he figures the door must be locked from the outside. With that he puts his head down, Rhobert begins to cry.

Bill picks up his phone and calls Christal, "Hey Christal, have you heard from Bud yet?" "No." she replies. "Are you busy right now?" asks Bill. "No." she replies. "Could you come over to my office please?" asks Bill. "Sure I will be right there." replies Christal hanging up. Bill hangs up his phone and waits for Christal. Christal knocks on Bill's door, "Come on in Christal, take a seat please." states Bill. "What's up Bill?" asks Christal. "Well Christal, Senator Daniel MacKenzie and Chief of Police are coming pretty soon today to approve and close the funding deal that also makes our Children's Home a Regional Youth Detention Center. They will have questions about our current status, are preparedness, can we handle the new task, and what plans for up-grade if any are needed do we have. They will also want a tour of our facilities as well. I am unable to contact Bud; he is not answering any of my phone calls." says Bill. "I know he is not answering any of my calls either." replies Christal. "Well Christal, this is not like Bud; especially with this important deal closing today. He must definitely be having some kind of trouble, to totally not show up today and not answer any of our phone calls. I have no other choice but to proceed without him, time is too short. I need to get myself up-to-speed and get prepared. I don't want us to look like a fool and risk losing this deal." says Bill. "What do you need from me Bill?" asks Christal. "Well Christal, I need you to bring me all of Bud's notes and files on the deal." requests Bill. "OK Bill, I will go get them and be right back." replies Christal as she gets up to leave. After a few minutes Christal comes back with a folder of papers and hands them to Bill. "Thank you Christal." says Bill. "I will be in my office if you need anything else Bill." says Christal. "Christal, if Bud gets here let me know, or when the others get here send them in to me." request Bill. "Sure will Bill." replies Christal as she was leaving Bill's office.

Adair carries a ladder to the solitary access door and sets it down, and leaves. He soon comes back with a box of assorted material, wearing a tool belt, and sets the box down by the solitary access door. He takes out the key, unlocks, and opens the door. He picks up the box of assorted material and sets it down off to the side at the top of the steps. He then goes out picks up the ladder stepping back inside the door, making sure that the door closes behind him. He then carefully carries the ladder down the steps to solitary; walking down the cubical aisle looking up at the ceiling to see where the heater air duct is. Once found, he leans the ladder against the back wall of the cubical, and then proceeds to go get the box of assorted material from the top of the steps. He comes back and sets the material box down in front of the ladder. Adair climbs the ladder, takes out a screw driver from the tool belt. He removes the screws holding the heater duct cover. With duct cover in hand, he climbs down the ladder setting the screws and cover down. He then climbs back up the ladder, taking a tape measure from the tool belt and measures the opening of the duct. He then climbs back down the ladder and opens the assorted material box. He pulls out a roll of thin insulation, measures and cuts four squares. He then pulls out a roll of rubber, measures and cuts five squares. Starting with the fifth rubber square, he then cuts one third from the top of the square and lays that square on the floor. He then places one of the four insulation squares on top of that rubber square. He then picks up the fourth rubber square and cuts one third from the bottom of the square and lays that square on top of the previous insulation square on the stack. This process continues until all nine pieces of squares are cut and properly stacked. With all the pieces stacked, he pulls out quick drying epoxy sealant and begins the process of sealing them together. While waiting for the epoxy to dry, Adair starts picking up all the left over pieces of material and puts them back into the box. He then carries the box back up to the top of the steps and goes back to the cubical. Once dry, Adair picks up the stack of material he made and carries it up the ladder fitting the stack into the heater duct. Satisfied he then climbs down the ladder, picks up the screws and duct cover, climbs back up the ladder, and screws the heater duct cover back in place. He climbs back down leaving the ladder in place, Adair leaves solitary making sure the door closes and locks behind him.

Adair goes to Bill's office and knocks on the door.

"What do you need Adair?" asks Bill. "Well sir, I have finished putting a noise baffle in the heater duct and wanted to test it with you." replies Adair. "Can I do it a little latter Adair, since Bud has not shown up today I am busy poring over these files before the Senator gets here?" asks Bill. "Sure we can Bill." replies Adair. Adair leaves, goes to the solitary access door, opens it, sets the box of material outside the door, and then he goes back down to solitary to get the ladder. He walks into the cubical where the ladder is, and grabs the ladder. As he carries the ladder out of the cubical not watching what he is doing; he bangs the ladder into a cubical wall. Unnoticed during the bang a small piece of metal the size of a needle flies from the ladder into Rhobert's cubical. Adair continues up the steps to leave solitary to return the ladder from where he got it. Adair returns to the solitary access door picks up the material box, and takes the box back from where he got it.

Ms. Aileen Anderson the Nurse arrives at the Belle Haute Children's Home and parks her car in the parking lot. She gets out of her car, locks the door, straightens her slacks, and begins to walk the sidewalk to the front door in the alcove. When she reaches the alcove she gets her keys to open the front door. Once inside she locks the door. She then proceeds to walk down the hall to the door labeled, "NURSES OFFICE," she unlocks the door and goes inside.

Rhobert gets on his knees and moves a little closer to the piece of metal that flew into his cubical. He reaches out and picks up the piece of metal, then moves back to the back wall and sits down. He places the tip of the metal into the lock of the shackle on his wrist and jimmies it around a bit. The lock on the shackle unlocks, and the shackle falls to the floor. Rhobert unlocks the remaining shackles, stands up and puts his clothes on. Rhobert checks his pocket for the cellar door key, and finds it is still there. He walks over to the cellar door, pulls out the key and unlocks the cellar door. Because of the caulk around the door, he has to pull hard to open it. Placing a foot against the wall for leverage, Rhobert pulls hard; the door pops open with a dull crack sound as the caulking gives way. Rhobert looks inside the door and is suddenly overcome by the deathly rotten smell. He throws up inside the door from the smell. When done, he quickly shuts the door taking deep breaths for air. He waits a minute to catch his breath. Rhobert then takes a deep breath in and holds it, opens the door and looks in. He sees and is shocked to find a half buried rotting decaying body covered with maggots. He looks beyond the decaying body and sees a small metal door that looks like an oven. He crawls to the small metal door and opens it, a small cloud of smoke and ash comes out. The bottom of the inside is covered with a pile of ashes. Rhobert rummages through the ashes and is surprised to find a set of small bones still attached to each other. Rhobert picks the bone up and it looks like a small finger. He puts the little finger bones in his pocket, closes the oven door, and starts to crawl out of the cellar. Once he is out he quickly shuts the cellar door stops holding his breath and breaths rapidly. Once he has caught his breath, Rhobert takes out the cellar key and locks the cellar door. He wipes all of the dirt off of his clothes onto the floor. Rhobert walks over to the closet door and opens it. He finds a dust pan and brush and then cleans up all of the dirt from off the floor. While emptying the dust pan into the trash can in the closet, Rhobert sees the caulking gun on a shelf. He puts the dust pan and brush down and grabs the caulking gun. Rhobert then caulks the cellar door, when he is finished he returns the caulking gun to the closet and shuts the closet door. Rhobert returns to his cubical, takes off his clothes hanging them back up, and then sits down putting his shackles back on. Tired and hungry he leans back against the cubical back wall to go back to waiting again, and to rest.

CHAPTER SIX

The local Priest, Father Mitchell Quinn, arrives at the Belle Haute Children's Home with two of his Nuns. The two Nuns are teachers for the Children's Home; Sister Diane Livingston teaches the boy's, and Sister Patricia Reeves teaches the girl's. The founders of Belle Haute Children's Home long ago arranged with the local diocese for two Nuns to teach the children of all ages at the Children's Home; one to teach the boy's and one to teach the girl's. Father Quinn parks his car in the parking lot. He and his two Nuns get out of his car and begin to walk the sidewalk to the front door in the alcove. Once at the door he presses the talk button on the speaker box. "Yes may I help you?" asks Ms. MacKenley the Headmaster's Secretary. "Yes you can Ms. MacKenley it is Father Quinn with Sister Livingston and Sister Reeves. Can you let us in please?" asks Father Quinn. "I sure can Father, be right there." replies Ms. MacKenley. Ms. MacKenley opens the door to let Father Quinn and the two Nuns inside.

They step inside the door while Ms. MacKenley makes sure that the door is locked back behind him. The two Nuns continue on to their classrooms, and Father Quinn remains behind for a moment. "Hello Ms. MacKenley, how are you this morning?" asks Father Quinn. "I am fine Father thank you for asking." replies Ms. MacKenley. "How are you today Father?" asks Ms. MacKenley. "I am blessed and highly favored." smiling replies Father Quinn. "Great. So what brings you out this morning Father?" asks Ms. MacKenley. "Well I am here to bless one of my boys." replies Father Quinn. "OK Father, go ahead on to Interview Room number one, and I will call Mr. Anderson to let him know to bring you one of the boys." replies Ms. MacKenley. "May God's blessings be on you my dear." says Father Quinn as he starts to head for the room.

Adair's office phone rings, Adair answers his phone, "Yea Mr. Anderson here." "Hey Adair, it's me Christal. Father Quinn is in Interview Room number one waiting for you to bring him a boy so he can bless him." says Christal. "Common Christal do not try to tell me you honestly believe that crap?" replies Adair. "Well Adair all I know is never question a man of the cloth doing the Lords work." replies Christal. "Yea right Christal. Don't piss down my back and try to tell me it's raining either." responds Adair hanging up the phone. The boy's who are done eating breakfast have come back to the Boy's Dormitory waiting for class to start. Adair goes out to send one of the boy's to Father Quinn, "Billy, Father

Quinn would like to see you in Interview Room number one. Go on now do not keep Father Quinn waiting." orders Adair. "Yes sir." replies Billy as he sadly sulks his way out of the dorm; as if he already knows what is in store for him. Some of the other boys in the dorm sadly look at each other with a sigh of relief; as if to say, "I am glad it was not me." Suddenly a loud bell rings throughout the Children's Home, indicating time for class to start. All the children start making their way to their class room.

On his way to Belle Haute Children's Home, Officer Brice Reid stops his patrol car outside the Maintenance Garage. He gets out of his patrol car and walks up to the window of the garage and looks inside. He sees his brother Torey sleeping on a cot in the garage. Officer Reid goes back to his patrol car and opens the trunk. He takes out a bullhorn, closing the trunk and walks back to the garage. He quietly opens the door and goes inside, shutting the door behind him. He sneaks up to Torey sleeping on the cot and puts the bullhorn near his head. Turning it on he speaks into it, "**TOREY REID, IT'S THE POLICE! COME OUT WITH YOUR HANDS UP!**" Arms and legs flapping and flailing Torey scrambles off the cot gets into a mean quick fighting stance. Brice is uncontrollably laughing at his brother's asinine reaction. Torey relaxes from his stance when he sees that it was just his brother playing a trick on him and yells, "Brice, you son of a bitch! That was not funny!" "You jumped like a scared bitch." still laughing replies Brice. "Ha Ha Ha, laugh it up. Why are you here Brice?" asks Torey. "I am here because the Senator is coming here today and I am in charge of security." replies Brice. "Yes, and I would bet you that if you were to look it up in your stupid cop book; that it does not say anything about using a bullhorn to wake your brother while being in charge of security either." says Torey. "Actually brother the book does say that. Officer's Handbook, Chapter Five, and Article Seven, paragraph two states: *…while precariously ascending upon a nefarious individual pernicious force to the extent necessary in order to thrall their attention is authorized!*" responds Brice trying hard to keep a straight face. "Yea right it really says that; shake this leg it plays jingle bells too." replies Torey. "Well Torey, I better get inside and get set up before they get here. Take care, I will talk with you later." says Brice. "All right Brice, see you." replies Torey.

Officer Reid walks out and gets into his patrol car and starts it up. He then drives to the parking lot of Belle Haute Children's Home. He gets out of his patrol car and walks the sidewalk to the front door in the alcove. Right before getting to the alcove, dispatch contacts him over his hand radio, "Patrol Nine." Officer Reid stops to respond, "Patrol Nine go ahead." "Patrol Nine C.O.P. (Chief of Police) and Senator are on their way E.T.A. (Estimated Time of Arrival) 25 min." reports dispatch. "Patrol Nine 10-4." replies Officer Reid. Officer Reid walks into the alcove and presses the talk button on the speaker box. "Yes, may I help you?" asks Ms. MacKenley. "Yes, Officer Reid here. I have a message for the Headmaster." replies Officer Reid. "Yes sir I will be right there." replies Ms.

MacKenley. Ms. MacKenley opens the Children's Home entrance door to let Officer Reid inside, then closes and locks the door and says, "Follow me, I will take you to the Assistant Headmaster." "No Ma'am I need to speak with the Headmaster." reports Officer Reid. "Well sir, the Headmaster is not with us yet today, and the Assistant Headmaster Mr. MacKenley will explain it all to you." replies Ms. MacKenley. "Well this better be good." retorts Officer Reid. Knowing there is nothing she can do or say about it, she takes Officer Reid to her brother's office. She stops and knocks on his office door stating, "Mr. MacKenley, Officer Reid is here to see you." Ms. MacKenley steps away leaving Officer Reid with her brother.

Finished cleaning the Children's Home, Doug goes back to the door labeled, "CLEANING LOCKER." He unlocks the door, opens it, and then pushes his cleaning cart into the space. He then logs his stop time on the time sheet, shuts and locks the door. Doug then makes his way to the exit door, takes out his key and unlocks it so he can leave. Stepping into the alcove he locks the door, and then he walks to his car, gets in, and leaves.

"Yes Officer Reid, what do you need of me? What can I do for you?" asks Mr. MacKenley. "Well sir I need to speak with the Headmaster." requests Officer Reid. "Well Officer Reid, he is not with us today; I am filling in for him. Therefore, whatever you need you can ask of me." orders Mr. MacKenley. "Well sir, the Chief of Police (C.O.P.) and the Senator are on their way here right now.

They will be here in fifteen minutes. I need you to have someone unlock the entrance door in the alcove. I will be standing guard outside in the alcove while the door remains unlocked so that the C.O.P. and Senator can leave without waiting. Is the Headmaster OK sir? Why is he not here today?" asks Officer Reid. "OK, Officer Reid thank you for letting me know. I will get the door unlocked when you are ready to go outside and wait. We currently do not know the whereabouts of the Headmaster Mr. Bud Dyer. He is not answering his home phone, or his cell phone when called. We have been calling him all morning long. Also his car is not at his home of residence." replies Mr. MacKenley. Officer Reid immediately speaks into his hand radio, "C.O.P., Patrol Nine." "Patrol Nine, C.O.P., Go ahead." blares out his radio. "C.O.P., Patrol Nine, be aware that the Headmaster Mr. Bud Dyer of Belle Haute Children's Home is not at work today, and the Assistant Headmaster Mr. MacKenley will be filling in for him." replies Officer Reid. "Patrol Nine, C.O.P., is there a reason why the Headmaster is unable to attend today's meeting?" asks over the radio. "C.O.P., Patrol Nine, unable to contact reason unknown." replies Officer Reid. "10-4 Patrol Nine." is the response over his radio. "Well sir, I am ready to go guard the door now." states Officer Reid. Mr. MacKenley picks up his phone and calls, "Yes Ms. MacKenley, could you please unlock the entrance door for Officer Reid and leave the door unlocked until the Senator is gone." directs Mr. MacKenley. "Yes sir, right away." replies Ms. MacKenley as she hangs up her phone going out to the entrance door. "She is on her way Officer Reid, you may go now," states Mr. MacKenley. Officer Reid leaves the office and walks to where Ms. MacKenley is waiting. Ms. MacKenley unlocks the door for Officer Reid. Officer Reid steps outside into the alcove and waits for the C.O.P. and Senator to arrive.

The Chief of Police, Captain Briar MacKenzie, arrives in a black unmarked sedan with black tinted windows, followed by the Senator's black SUV with black tinted windows. Officer Reid presses the talk button on the speaker box, and announces their arrival, "Attention everyone the Chief of Police and the Senator are here." Mr. MacKenley walks out of his office on his way to the alcove to greet the Senator. Ms. MacKenley is standing by her office door, as Mr. MacKenley passes her he tells her, "Turn on the Headmaster's Office light and make sure the conference table is ready." Mr. MacKenley joins Officer Reid in the alcove. Captain MacKenzie, followed by Senator Daniel MacKenzie arrive at the alcove; Captain MacKenzie steps to the side to let the Senator pass him. The Senator approaches Mr. MacKenley. Mr. MacKenley extends a hand to shake hands with the Senator and says, "Good afternoon, welcome to Belle Haute Children's Home Senator MacKenzie." Senator MacKenzie shakes hands, "Thank you, good afternoon Mr. MacKenley." "Gentlemen if you will come with me please." requests Mr. MacKenley. He leads them into the Headmaster's Office to the large conference room table. Ms. MacKenley is standing by the coffee maker with three cups of coffee on a tray. Mr. MacKenley stands at the head of the table waiting for Senator MacKenzie and Captain MacKenzie to take their seat. The conference room table on the left and right side of Mr. MacKenley both has copies of briefs prepared by Mr. MacKenley. They both go to their seat, and everyone sits down. Ms. MacKenley takes the coffee to the gentlemen at the table then goes to stand by the door. Once seated Senator MacKenzie begins to speak, "Well Mr. MacKenley let me start by saying that I am sorry to hear that Mr. Dyer is predisposed today and could not make this meeting. Like you, we hope all is well with him. My office stands ready to help if needed. You also know why I am here. I am here to review and examine the Children's Home preparedness and readiness for the pending appointment as a Regional Youth Detention Center. Even without Mr. Dyer here, I am positive that you are well aware, knowledgeable of all facets involved, and capable for the task at hand. I am willing to proceed without Mr. Dyer; unless you would prefer to reschedule this meeting?" "Thank you, Senator and Captain MacKenzie. I will keep you both informed on Mr. Dyer's disposition, and if needed I will contact you for help. I am prepared to proceed without Mr. Dyer; therefore, we do not need to reschedule. I feel that I am highly qualified to speak for the entire Children's Home today." replies Mr. MacKenley. "Very well then, let us get started." states Senator MacKenzie.

Father Quinn walks up to the exit, surprised to learn that it is currently unlocked. He walks out into the alcove where Officer Reid is standing. Father Quinn steps around Officer Reid asking, "Hello Officer Reid is everything OK?" "Oh yes Father, Senator MacKenzie is here." replies Officer Reid. "Well good bye and God bless you my son. Have a safe day." says Father Quinn. "Thank you Father." replies Officer Reid.

"Mr. MacKenley can you please state the current condition, strengths and weaknesses of Belle Haute Children's Home?" requests Senator MacKenzie. "Yes sir. As stated in our previous letter of assessment, the Belle Haute Children's Home was founded fifty years ago by the local Catholic diocese, then later sold to private enterprise due to lack of funds. The Children's Home was built with sound metal, brick, and cement foundation. All outside windows are enclosed with wire mesh, and their exterior covered with steel bars to prevent break in, and break out. The Children's Home does not currently employ the use of any security guards; nor does it have any security equipment, such as security cameras and recording devices. The main reason for that is because most all of the exit doors, with a couple exceptions, are locked from the outside and also from the inside. This keeps out those that we don't need in, and those that don't need out. Only the staff is given a key to the locked exit doors to come and go for work. The couple exceptions are the exit door just outside the Girl's Dormitory and Boy's Dormitory. These two doors open into the large backyard of the Children's Home which is completely surrounded by a twelve foot high brick wall topped with barbed wire. They are open from the inside, and locked from the outside to keep out anyone who has been able to scale the brick wall from the outside.

The Children's Home currently employs nine people; seven of them are full-time, and two of them are part-time. The full-time positions are: the Administrator/Headmaster, the Assistant Administrator/Headmaster, the Headmaster's Secretary, the House Mother – person in charge of the Girl's Dormitory, the House Father – person in charge of the Boy's Dormitory, the Cook, and the Maintenance Grounds Technician. The two part-time positions are: the Janitor, and the Nurse. We are currently considering making the Maintenance Grounds Keeper a part-time position. The founders of Belle Haute Children's Home also arranged with the local diocese, and that arrangement is still in effect today; at no expense to the Children's Home to have two Nuns report to the Children's Home to teach when school is scheduled. One Nun will teach the Girl's and one Nun will teach the Boy's. I would at this time like to point out that should Belle Haute Children's Home ever lose this arrangement with the diocese; then schooling of the children would involve making arrangements, to include transportation to and from, with the local schooling community and managed by the Department of Children Family Services (DCFS).

The Belle Haute Children's Home has a current twenty single bed capacity for both the Girl's and the Boy's Dormitories; a total of 40 children of various ages.

The capacity break down is currently twenty for the Girl's Dormitory, and twenty for the Boy's Dormitory. Children eighteen and over are no longer "Ward's of the State," and therefore are not kept by the Children's Home. Girl's Dormitory is currently housing seventeen girls, and the Boy's Dormitory is currently housing twelve boys. As previously stated, the capacities for the Girl's and Boy's Dormitories are single bed capacities; these capacities could be doubled by replacing single beds with bunk beds if necessary. Due to their position with the Children's Home, the House Mother and House Father both have single bed in their office.

This concludes my deposition on the current condition of the Belle Haute Children's Home. I would be glad to answer any questions that you may have." concludes Mr. MacKenley. "Chief do you have any questions for Mr. MacKenley?" asked Senator MacKenzie. "No sir I do not." replies Chief of Police, Captain Briar MacKenzie. "If it is OK with you gentlemen, let's take a five minute recess." states Senator MacKenzie. "OK, that is fine." replies both Mr. MacKenley and Captain MacKenzie. Everyone stands to let the Senator leave first, followed by Captain MacKenzie. Christal comes into the Headmaster's Office and asks in a low voice, "So how did it go Bill? Are you done?" "So far so good Christal, and no we are not done yet. Any word from Bud?" replies and asks Bill. "No he still is not answering his phones." replies Christal. The Senator and Chief of Police begin to make their way back into the room. Christal takes a pot of coffee around and asks,

"Captain MacKenzie would you like some more coffee?" "Yes please." responds Captain MacKenzie. After pouring more coffee for the Captain, Christal goes to the Senator and asks, "Senator would you like some more coffee?" "No thank you Ms. MacKenley." responds the Senator. Christal sets the coffee pot on the burner on her way back to her office. The Senator walks over to Mr. MacKenly and asks, "Any word on Mr. Dyer?" "Still no word Senator." replies Mr. MacKenley. "Any idea why?" asks Senator MacKenzie. "No sir this is highly unusual of him, and honestly I am beginning to fear the worst." replies Mr. MacKenley. "Chief?" asks Senator MacKenzie directing the question to Captain MacKenzie. "Already on it; I have issued a B.O.L.O. (Be On the Look Out) for Mr. Bud Dyer sir." replies Captain MacKenzie. "Very good Chief, keep me informed." directs Senator MacKenzie. "Mr. MacKenley, just so that you know, should Mr. Bud Dyer never return for whatever reason. I am personally going to appoint his replacement." states Senator MacKenzie. "May I ask who you have in mind Senator?" asks Mr. MacKenley. "Yes you can Mr. MacKenley I have every intention of appointing my brother Mr. Tavin MacKenzie he has years of previous experience in running a Youth Detention Center." replies Senator MacKenzie. Everyone takes their seat, and Senator MacKenzie starts the meeting again, "OK gentlemen let us continue on. Mr. MacKenley could you please describe for us the Children's Home's preparedness, ability to take on the task of Regional Youth Detention Center, and any plans for upgrade that may be needed to take on this new task." states Senator MacKenzie.

Mr. MacKenley begins, "Yes sir. As previously shown the Belle Haute Children's Home is already a secure residential facility for young people. We fully understand that Juvenile detention is not intended to be punitive, but rather a secure safe place to receive care consistent with doctrine. Making Belle Haute Children's Home responsible for providing education, recreation, health, assessment, counseling and other intervention services with the intent of maintaining a youth's well-being during his or her stay in custody. We also realize that most of detained juveniles that will be placed here at Belle Haute Children's Home are going to be considered a threat to public safety, a party to the court process, or held for violating a court order. It is for that reason we would recommend a separate and secure berthing facility be added to Belle Haute. This new facility should be built with the consideration that it would berth both the girls and the boys separately. This new facility should also be built with the consideration that it would have a maximum berthing capacity of forty each. This new facility should also include: an office for security personnel, an office for a nurse, an office for DCFS personnel, an office for the designated House Father, and an office for the designated House Mother. If our current design recommendations for this facility are approved; then the facility would be built off of one of the three brick walls surrounding the Children's Home backyard.

If Belle Haute Children's Home is approved to take on the additional pending task of Regional Youth Detention Center; then the following full-time and part-time positions would be recommended: seven full-time security personnel one in charge, three security personnel for the Girl's, and also three security personnel for the Boys', a part-time security trained nurse, a full-time security trained House Father, and a full-time security trained House Mother. We also recommend that a second full-time security trained Youth Detention Center Assistant Headmaster to the Headmaster be added to personnel employed at Belle Haute Children's Home. In addition, including the new facility if approved, the entire Belle Haute Children's Home and Youth Detention Center should have a security camera system installed.

This will conclude my assessment of Belle Haute Children's Home being considered for the addition of a Regional Youth Detention Center. I will answer any questions you may have." concludes Mr. MacKenley. The Senator asks, "Chief do you have any questions for Mr. MacKenley?" "Yes sir I do." replies Captain MacKenzie. "Go ahead then Chief." states Senator MacKenzie. "Mr. MacKenley, have you ever lost any children at Belle Haute Children's Home at any time, by means of escaping, or running away?" asks Captain MacKenzie. "Since the Children's Home changed its policy that all of the exit doors will be locked inside and out; the Belle Haute Children's Home has not ever lost one child by means of escaping, or running away." replies Mr. MacKenley.

"Mr. MacKenley when was the Belle Haute Children's Home exit door policy was changed?" asked Captain MacKenzie. "The founders changed that policy a few years after the Children's Home was built, fifty years ago." replies Mr. MacKenley. There is a short pause at the table. "Chief anymore questions for Mr. MacKenley?" asked Senator MacKenzie. "No sir, I do not have any more questions for Mr. MacKenley at this time." replies Captain MacKenzie.

"Alright, Mr. MacKenley that was a remarkably amazing job convincing us that the Belle Haute Children's Home is ready and knowledgeable to accept the task of becoming the new Regional Youth Detention Center. I hereby authorize and approve a 2.5 million dollar funding package for the addition of the new Regional Youth Detention Center to the Belle Haute Children's Home. In so doing Mr. MacKenley you may begin the process of fielding bids for the construction of the new Regional Youth Detention Center. Also, Mr. MacKenley you may begin the interviewing of qualified applications process for additional personnel to staff the new Regional Youth Detention Center. Finally Mr. MacKenley, I am hereby terminating as of right now Mr. Bud Dyer as Headmaster with prejudice due to his unacceptable absence from work. I am appointing the highly qualified and experienced trained Mr. Tavin MacKenzie as the new Administrator/Headmaster of Belle Haute Children's Home and the new Regional Youth Detention Center. I trust Mr. MacKenley that you will give him the same respect and brief that you have just gave me. We can fore-go the tour if no one objects. That is all gentlemen." concludes Senator MacKenzie. They stand up and shake hands, and begin to walk out of the office.

"Hello welcome back. Julie Fox of KSAP coming to you live at the Belle Haute Children's Home with an update on the story that we have been covering. Senator MacKenzie is here at the Belle Haute Children's Home to assess their ability to take on the role of becoming the new Regional Youth Detention Center for our area. The Belle Haute children's Home can currently house a maximum of 40 children. We are told that the maximum amount could be changed to 80 if Belle Haute Children's Home was to replace the current single beds with bunk beds. I am also told that if the Senator approves Belle Haute Children's Home for becoming the new Regional Youth Detention Center; Belle Haute Children's Home would receive a 2.5 million dollar funding package to build the new Youth Detention Center annex. The new annex could house a maximum amount of 80 children. The new annex would employee twelve more people. OK, I just got word they are finished with the assessment, and they are on their way out. Here he comes now." Senator MacKenzie walks up to the microphone, "Good afternoon. This afternoon, after a thorough review I am designating Belle Haute Children's Home the new Regional Youth Detention Center. I have approved a 2.5 million dollar funding package for Belle Haute Children's Home to build the new Regional Youth Detention Center. I also have appointed Mr. Tavin MacKenzie as new Administrator/ Headmaster of Belle Haute Children's Home to oversee the construction of the new Regional Youth Detention Center." Senator MacKenzie begins to walk away Julie Fox walks up to him with her microphone and camera crew, "Senator MacKenzie, isn't this just another one of your family's scam tactic's to milk the local government for some more money?" "No comment." replies Senator MacKenzie. Captain MacKenzie rushes up and pushes Julie Fox away, "The Senator is not answering any questions at this time." Julie Fox pushes Captain MacKenzie aside, "Out of my way monkey boy." and yells after the Senator, "Senator MacKenzie is it not true that your office ordered the death of Mr. Bud Dyer so that you could appoint your brother as the new Headmaster of Belle Haute Children's Home to oversee the money so that you could line your pockets?"

CHAPTER SEVEN

Father Mitchell Quinn returns to Belle Haute Children's Home to pick up the two Nuns. He parks his car, gets out, and begins to walk towards the front entrance in the alcove. He notices that Officer Brice Reid is gone. When he gets to the front door he presses the talk button on the speaker box to announce his presence. "Yes may I help you?" asks Christal. "Yes Ms. MacKenley it is me again Father Quinn I am would like to come inside." replies Father Quinn. "Yes Father Quinn I will be right there." says Christal. Christal unlocks and opens the door for Father Quinn. Father Quinn steps inside the door, while Christal locks the door behind him; but Christal no sooner locks the door when the school bell rings, announcing that school is over. Shortly afterwards, Sister Livingston and Sister Reeves join Father Quinn who is waiting at the door. Christal unlocks the door to let them out and they all leave, as soon as they leave Christal locks the door and returns to her office.

As Father Quinn with the two Nuns is pulling out of the parking lot to Belle Haute Children's Home, Mrs. MacQuire from DCFS pulls into the parking lot. She gets out of her car, locks the door, and begins to walk to the front entrance door in the alcove. When she gets to the front door she presses the talk button on the speaker box. "Yes may I help you?" asks Christal. "Yes this is Mrs. MacQuire from DCFS. I am here to see Rhobert Rodriguez." replies Mrs. MacQuire. "Yes Mrs. MacQuire I will be right there," replies Christal. Christal unlocks and opens the door for Mrs. MacQuire, as Mrs. MacQuire steps in through the open door Christal locks the door. "Mrs. MacQuire please wait right here and I will have Rhobert brought to you." says Christal. Christal goes into her office and calls Adair, "Yes Adair Mrs. MacQuire from DCFS is here to see Rhobert." "OK thank you Christal give me a couple minutes." says Adair.

Ms. Aileen Anderson leaves her office, locks the door and starts walking towards the exit door to leave. On her way, her brother Adair rushes past her, "Hi sis, sorry I can't stay and talk for a bit. I am in a hurry." "That is OK, we can talk later. I have got to run anyway." says Aileen. Aileen makes it to the exit door where Mrs. MacQuire is waiting. "Hello Ms. Anderson how are you today?" asks Mrs. MacQuire. "Just fine now that my day is done." replies Aileen. "Well that is good." says Mrs. MacQuire. "Have a good day." says Aileen as she unlocks the exit door and leaves.

Adair quickly goes down the hallway to the locked

door labeled, "STORAGE ONLY NOT AN EXIT." He unlocks the door and goes down into solitary stopping at the closet door. He opens the closet door and gets the nozzle end of the garden hose, and turns on the water. He then goes to Rhobert's cubical and begins spraying down Rhobert's dirty naked body to clean him up. Making sure Rhobert is clean he unlocks the chains from Rhobert. He tosses Rhobert a towel and says, "Dry off and get dressed." Rhobert dries himself off and takes his clothes off of the hook and puts them on. Adair opens up the closet door, turns off the water, and rolls the hose back up. He closes the closet door and tells Rhobert, "Let's go." They exit solitary Rhobert starts to head for the Boy's Dormitory, and Adair says to Rhobert, "No this way." Adair takes Rhobert to the front door where Mrs. MacQuire is waiting to see him. "Hello Rhobert." says Mrs. MacQuire. She turns and asks Adair, "Mr. Anderson, is there somewhere in here that Rhobert and I can go for some privacy?" Bill steps out of his office and responds, "Yes here you go Mrs. MacQuire you may use my office." "Thank you very much Mr. MacKenley." replies Mrs. MacQuire.

Mrs. MacQuire takes Rhobert into Mr. MacKenley's office and closes the door. They both sit down, then Mrs. MacQuire asks Rhobert, "How have you been Rhobert?" "Not good." says Rhobert. "Why not good Rhobert?" asks Mrs. MacQuire. "Because I tried to run away and got caught so they chained me naked to the wall in this cement cube in the basement without food or water for the past day." replies Rhobert. "Oh my Rhobert."

responds Mrs. MacQuire. "Tell me Rhobert, why did you try to run away?" asked Mrs. MacQuire. "Because that House man he is mean and evil. He beats us with his cane pole. He yells at us, and makes us call him sir." says Rhobert. "The House Father, Mr. Anderson does that?" asks Mrs. MacQuire, beginning to think Rhobert's story may have some relevance. "Yes that's the man." replies Rhobert. "Well then, I will have to have a talk with the Headmaster about all of this right away Rhobert." states Mrs. MacQuire, thinking to herself that solves that. "No please you cannot do that. Do not tell the Headmaster." demands Rhobert. "How come I cannot just go to the Headmaster and clear everything up Rhobert?" asks Mrs. MacQuire, wondering how come Rhobert is making this simple matter complicated. "Because they will definitely kill you and then they will kill me." says Rhobert. "Oh Rhobert I assure you they will not kill us." replies Mrs. MacQuire. "Yes they will, they already have killed." states Rhobert. "What are you talking about Rhobert?" asks Mrs. MacQuire, now he has my attention. "When I tried to run away, I ran out of the exit door by the Boy's Dormitory the door closed. I was locked out and I could not get back in. I was in this huge backyard that had really high walls all the way around the backyard. I did not want to press the talk button on the speaker box to get back in. That is when I met this girl from the Girl's Dormitory named Carla Ashton. She put something down to block the door to keep it from closing and locking her out, and then she came into the backyard. She went to go by the tree to pray. She told me she was praying for her sister. They killed Carla's sister after she tried to run away, and they also killed the lady who the sister ran away to telling her what was going on here. They buried them both by the tree. So every night Carla goes out in the backyard after everyone goes to sleep to pray for her sister." says Rhobert. "Yes, I remember that girl's disappearance several years ago. How does Carla know that they buried her sister and that woman by the tree?" asks Mrs. MacQuire. "Because Carla watched them bury them both, that's how." replies Rhobert. "Is that all you were going to tell me Rhobert?" asks Mrs. MacQuire. "No, after a while outside, Carla and I both went back into the Children's Home through that blocked open Girl's Dormitory exit door. Carla went back to the Girl's Dormitory and I went down the hall to go back to the Boy's Dormitory. On the way, I passed two doors that were labeled INTERVIEW ROOM ONE and INTERVIEW ROOM TWO. Both of the doors were unlocked so I peaked inside. In both of the rooms there was a mattress on the floor without sheets or covers, and both rooms had some foam with cones covering all the walls from top to bottom. Then on my way back to the Boy's Dormitory I saw the House man and some guy in fatigues, the same one I saw after I heard that girl crying begging for someone to stop." interrupted, Rhobert stops talking. "What do you mean you heard a girl crying begging for someone to stop Rhobert?" asks Mrs. MacQuire. "That night, that you brought me here to this Children's Home, and you had me wait on the bench.

I heard a voice coming from the heater duct by the bench. The voice I heard was a girl crying and begging someone to stop. Then I heard a thud and she quit crying." says Rhobert. "Oh my God Rhobert, that is so awful." replies Mrs. MacQuire.

"OK Rhobert, what were you going to tell me about those two guys?" asked Mrs. MacQuire. "Yes, I saw them carrying a large bag with something heavy in it out into the backyard at the far right corner. Then I immediately went and got into my bed. One of them came back inside to go get some shovels. I heard him come back with the shovels, and go back outside. I got out of bed and went to go look outside the exit door window, and I saw both of them digging a big hole in the ground. That morning when I woke up the House man took me down to the basement. Made me take off all of my clothes, and he put chains on both of my hands and feet. I stole a key to this little door that was locked. I picked the locks of the chains that were on me and got free. Then I went to see what was behind that little door, why it was being locked. I opened that little door and oh my God it smelt so very bad in there. I saw this half buried rotting body with maggots all over it. Then I saw a metal oven in the far back side. So I crawled to the oven, opened it and I found this." says Rhobert as he reaches into his pocket and gives the bones that looks like a finger and the key to the little door to Mrs. MacQuire. "Then I crawled out, locked the little door, went and put my chains back on. After a very long time down there in that cold basement, you come and they let me go." says Rhobert. "Rhobert, I need to get you somewhere so you will be safe, away from here." states Mrs. MacQuire. "No Mrs. MacQuire, they will kill us both then." says Rhobert. "Trust me Rhobert, no one will kill us." replies Mrs. MacQuire. "Wait here Rhobert, I will be right back." states Mrs. MacQuire. Mrs. MacQuire goes into the Headmaster's Secretary's Office.

Mr. Tavin MacKenzie, the new Administrator/Headmaster, arrives at Belle Haute Children's Home and parks his car in his designated parking spot. He gets out of his vehicle, locks the door, then he begins to walk the sidewalk to the entrance door in the alcove. Once at the door, he takes out his key, and goes inside. He walks in the Headmaster's Secretary's Office where Bill and Mrs. MacQuire are arguing, "No, Mrs. MacQuire, you cannot take Rhobert and Carla with you away from the Children's Home this late in the day." argues Bill. "You will bring Carla Ashton to me, and you will bring both Rhobert's and Carla's street clothes to me too, or DCFS will make your life a pure hell Mr. MacKenley." demands Mrs. MacQuire. "No I will not let you take." continues arguing Bill, when suddenly he is interrupted by Tavin. "**THAT IS ENOUGH!!!**" yells Tavin. Surprised everyone shuts up, and turns their focus on an individual that neither one of them have never met or seen before. Tavin turns to Christal and orders her, "Ms. MacKenley you will kindly go call the House Mother Mrs. Gaven and direct her to bring Carla Ashton and Carla's street clothes to Mrs. MacQuire. Then you will call the House Father Mr. Anderson and direct him to bring Rhobert's street clothes to Mrs. MacQuire as well. And you of all people, Mr. MacKenley, you will get the hell out of my Secretary's Office, go stand your ass by the exit door, and you will wait there until Rhobert Rodriguez, Carla Ashton, and Mrs. MacQuire are ready to leave. At which time you will unlock the exit door to let them out to leave, do you understand me?" demands Tavin. "Just who the hell do you think you are? No one off the street can just be-bop in here pretty as you please and start bossing my people around. How the hell did you get in here to begin with anyway?" demands an upset Bill. "Oh please forgive me. I am so very sorry, how rude of me. Please, allow me to introduce myself. I am Mr. Tavin MacKenzie the new Administrator/Headmaster of both the Belle Haute Children's Home and the new Regional Youth Detention Center; and oh yes, **YOUR WORST NIGHTMARE** you stupid idiot. These are my people, not yours. Now get the hell out of my Secretary's Office, and start doing pretty as you please as I have instructed you to do. Do you understand me Mr. MacKenley?" demands Tavin with an evil glare. "Yes sir." shaking responds Bill as he leaves to go stand by the exit door. He then turns his evil glare on Christal, "Yes sir." trembling responds Christal as she picks up her phone and starts to call.

Tavin then turns and extends his hand out to shake hands with Mrs. MacQuire, "I am so very sorry for that burst of disrespect Mrs. MacQuire. I will absolutely make sure that it does not ever happen again." says Tavin. Mrs. MacQuire shakes his hand and asks, "Wow! What have I missed here?" "You really honestly do not know, do you? Well please step into my office Mrs. MacQuire." says Tavin. They both go into the Headmaster's Office, taking a seat as Tavin begins to explain to Mrs. MacQuire, "Earlier this afternoon, Senator MacKenzie selected the Belle Haute Children's Home to also become the new Regional Youth Detention Center approving a 2.5 million dollar funding package to start building a new annex that will be the new Regional Youth Detention Center. It will have a maximum 80 youth capacity when it is completed. Headmaster Mr. Bud Dyer was terminated as Headmaster due to his absence from this very important meeting. He was slated to be terminated anyway because with the new Regional Youth Detention Center, the Headmaster needs to have the security training and experience of running a Youth Detention Center. I was appointed to be his replacement, which explains my appearance here now. I am very glad that I showed up here when I did to help alleviate what could have been a messy situation." "Thank you Mr. MacKenzie, now if you will excuse me I really have got to get back to Rhobert. He is waiting for me and he is probably scared." says Mrs. MacQuire. "Yes of course, I'm very sorry, please forgive me. I really did not mean to keep you Mrs. MacQuire. Mrs. MacQuire, I will call you later on to arrange a meeting with you about our new plans for the Regional Youth Detention Center that will involve DCFS. Also Mrs. MacQuire, just so that you know, you will bring those two children back to Belle Haute Children's Home when you are finished with whatever it is that you are taking them for. Otherwise, I will have you arrested and charged with abduction and Kidnapping. Do I make myself clear Mrs. MacQuire? Good day Mrs. MacQuire." kindly replies Tavin. Upset and mad about what the Tavin so arrogantly concluded their conversation with; Mrs. MacQuire angrily leaves that office without even one word.

Standing at the door of the Headmaster's Office through the latter half of their conversation, Christal steps aside to let the Mrs. MacQuire pass. "Yes Ms. MacKenley what do you need?" asks Tavin. "Yes sir, I just wanted to let you know that I contacted Mrs. Gaven and Mr. Anderson as you requested." replies Christal. "Thank you Ms. MacKenley you may go now." replies Tavin. "Also Ms. MacKenley, do not ever let me catch you standing in the door of my office when I am having a meeting with anyone, or I will definitely terminate your employment. Do I make myself clear?" demands Tavin. "Yes sir." says Christal as she leaves the Headmaster's Office shaken up almost in tears.

Mrs. MacQuire goes back into Bill's office where Rhobert is and tries to calm herself down. "Are you OK, what is the matter Mrs. MacQuire?" asks Rhobert. "Yes Rhobert, I am fine, do not worry." says Mrs. MacQuire. Someone knocks and then opens the door. "Excuse me Mrs. MacQuire I have Carla Ashton and her street clothes for you." states Mrs. Gaven. "Thank you." replies

Mrs. MacQuire as Carla Ashton steps into the office. Mrs. Gaven closes the door and goes back to the Girl's Dormitory. "Hello Carla, I am Mrs. Sandra MacQuire from DCFS. Rhobert was telling me about your sister Lynn. I was around when they said she was missing. I am very sorry to learn that these people killed her. I see that you have your street clothes, so please go ahead and put them on for me. Rhobert and I will turn around for you." states Mrs. MacQuire. Rhobert and Mrs. MacQuire turn around to let Carla put on her street clothes. "OK I am done." says Carla, Rhobert and Mrs. MacQuire turn back around. Another knock on the door and the door opens, "Here are Rhobert's street clothes you asked for." states Adair, as he hands over Rhobert's street clothes. Rhobert takes his clothes from Adair, and Adair shuts the door and leaves. Carla and Mrs. MacQuire turn around to let Rhobert put his street clothes on. When he is done Rhobert says, "OK I am done." Carla and Mrs. MacQuire turn back around. "OK you two stay with me, we will all leave together." says Mrs. MacQuire. She opens the door to leave and they all walk over to where Bill is waiting to let them out. Bill unlocks and opens the exit door for them so that they may all leave. They leave to go get into Mrs. MacQuire's car without either one of them saying one word to Bill. Mrs. MacQuire unlocks the car doors, and the three of them get into the car. Mrs. MacQuire starts the car and pulls out of the parking lot. After they are undoubtedly gone Bill closes and locks the exit door; then furiously returns to his office slamming the door shut behind him. Irritably trying to stop thinking about how humiliating the new Headmaster treated him and made him feel.

Christal steps into her brother's office, "Hey are you OK?" she asks shutting the door. "Oh my God he is such a arrogant pompous ass," replies Bill. "He just slips right in out of nowhere like some sneaky king snake, and takes over my job. Ten years of all that hard work doing the damn work of the Headmaster sucking hind tit, all down the drain. I was supposed to be promoted not him damn it. He comes in first thing he does is rub it in my face, humiliating me in front of others." complains Bill. "Oh brother I am so sorry," replies Christal. "I know what you mean though, because he threatened to fire me. I did not want to tell you." continues Christal. "Oh no he did not do that!" says Bill. "That son-of-a-bitch, if he fires you, then I am going to go with you. He can find some other monkey to do his work for him." responds Bill. "Oh Bill no, you like your job." replies Christal. "I used to Christal." responds Bill. "Well Bill lets go home I will cook you some supper." replies Christal. "OK that sounds like a really good idea sis." agrees Bill. "Alright I will go get my purse and meet you at the exit door." responds Christal as she leaves Bill's office.

Grabbing her cell phone, Mrs. Sandra MacQuire calls her brother's cell phone, "Hey David do you remember that you told me if I ever got you some hard solid proof about any deaths or murders of children at the Belle Haute Children's Home that I should call you?" asks

Sandra. "Yes I do sis, why do you have something for me now?" asks Mr. David MacQuire, a Special Agent of the Federal Bureau of Investigation (FBI) in Virginia. "Yes David, I have the bone fragment of a finger of the remains of a child. Two children who are witnesses of death and buried remains at the Children's Home." says Sandra. "OK Sandra let me run this by my boss, and I will catch the next plane out." responds David.

CHAPTER EIGHT

Torey leaves the Maintenance Garage and heads over to the main building. He goes inside and checks Bill's office door to see if Bill is in, and he finds that the door to Bill's office locked. He then goes across the hall to see if Christal is in. He steps into Christal's Office and Tavin yells for him, "Hey Mr. Reid could I have a word?" Torey steps up to the door to Mr. MacKenzie's Office, "Maybe, just who the hell are you and why are you in this office? No one is allowed to be in this office?" asks Torey. "I am the new Administrator/Headmaster, Mr. Reid it is quite alright. Please come inside and take a seat." says Tavin. Torey guardedly goes into the Headmaster's Office and takes a seat. "Cup of coffee?" asks Tavin. "Sure," replies Torey. Tavin hands Torey a fresh cup of coffee. "Thank you." says Torey. "Earlier today, Senator MacKenzie terminated Mr. Bud Dyer as the Headmaster, and then he appointed me as the new Administrator/Headmaster of Belle Haute Children's Home and also the new Regional Youth

Detention Center. He also approved a funding package to begin construction on the new Youth Detention Center annex, and that Mr. Reid, is why I called you in here. I would like to know if you would have any contractor recommendations?" asks Tavin. "This new annex that you are talking about building, what is the maximum youth capacity will it hold?" asks Torey. "Well what we are planning is for both dormitories to hold no more than 40 boys and 40 girls. Like the Children's Home, with the new annex the dormitories will be separated. We will also need to have five offices with this new annex: one for the person in charge of the boys off the boy's dormitory, one for the person in charge of the girls off the girl's dormitory, an office for the security personnel, an office for the Nurse, and an office for general use too. Also, both this annex and the Children's Home will have new security camera equipment installed." replies Tavin. "Sir with all due respect do not put the horse before the chart. You do not need a contractor, what you need is a Project Manager. A good Project Manager serves as your agent, and coordinates all the construction working within your budget. He will manage the entire construction through to completion, coordinating all subcontractor bidding activities, manage material procurement, monitor costs, and he will maintain quality control and safety standards. He will resolve any outstanding issues, and oversee any new system and equipment operation training. He will communicate with you providing you periodic status reports; and you control the periodicity of those reports."

states Torey. "That is an excellent idea, exactly what I am looking for. Thank you very much." agrees Tavin. Torey stands up to leave, "Your welcome, I am glad that I could help." replies Torey. Torey leaves the Headmaster's Office and goes to the exit door. He unlocks the exit door, steps out and locks it back up then walks back to the Maintenance Garage.

The Senator's wife Elizabeth is a petite and very beautiful woman looking like a fashion model right off the run way. Light green eye's and thin fine hair cut evenly just a couple inches above the shoulder. She is a very wise and headstrong woman who fervently always stands by the Senator's side for nearly twenty eight years. Devoted wife, mother, daughter, and grandmother, she is constantly looking for ways to love, share, and have fun. Senator MacKenzie's personal telephone line rings, he answers it, "Hello." "Hello Danny boy." says the voice on the phone. "Who are you, what do you want, and just how the hell did you get this number?" asks Dan. "Irrelevant Danny boy, what is relevant is that you are going to have your brother Tavin at the Children's Home hire a mutual friend of ours; an ex-Navy Seal as the leader of the security for the new Detention Center, or else." demands the voice on the phone. Dan hangs up the telephone. The telephone rings again, and Elizabeth answers the phone, she brings the phone to her husband, "Honey, it is for you, your friend he states that the call was just interrupted." says Elizabeth as she hands the phone to Dan. "OK Danny boy, let's try this again shall we. Once again, you are going to do as I say, or the envelope that is at your door goes public. Go ahead, go get the envelope. You had better hurry, go get it and look inside before Elizabeth gets a hold of it. It is OK I will wait." says the voice on the phone. Dan quickly goes to the door retrieves the envelope, opens up the envelope looking inside and he finds several pictures. He takes a look at the pictures that are inside the envelope and quickly puts them back into the envelope so that Elizabeth does not see them. Dan picks up the phone, "If these go public I will kill you!" yells Dan. "Now come on Danny boy, do not be an idiot. We both know very well that you are in no position to do that; besides, look around, you are the one on the short end of the stick. Now Dan you really need to write this down if you cannot keep up. You will have your brother hire the ex-Navy Seal as leader for the security for the Detention Center, or else I will go public with all of these photos. Also, just for fun I will mail copies to Elizabeth. Danny boy, I am very positive that Elizabeth would just love to see pictures of you having intercourse with an unwilling twelve year old from the Children's Home. Come to think of it, I am also pretty certain that there are a couple laws that are being broken here too," says the voice on the phone. "Look damn it, I am warning you," responds Dan, as he is interrupted. "OK Dan I am done playing around with you now. You will do as I have instructed, or else the news, the police, and Elizabeth will all find out," states the voice as he hangs up the phone on Dan.

Still infuriated about last night's telephone call, Dan

calls his brother Tavin at the Children's Home, "Hey brother it is me Dan. I found someone that I want you to hire as the leader of security for the new Detention Center. He is an ex-Navy Seal, an excellent choice for the position." states Dan. "That sounds good Dan thank you. I will give it some thought." replies Tavin. "Well brother that is why I am calling, I am not asking you to hire him. I am telling you that you will hire him." demands Dan. "Whoa, wait just a minute there Dan. You put me here to do a job, so back off and let me do the job. I do not need you to tell me how to do my job." argues Tavin. "I am not telling you how to do your job Tavin. Just do this one thing for me!" demands Dan. "Well since you put it like that Dan, we are back to where we started. I will think about it." responds Tavin. "Look Tavin let me put it to you another way then. Hire this guy, or I will cut the funding for the Youth Detention Center and replace you with the Assistant Headmaster." demands Dan. "Well Dan, since you put it like that. I guess that if I want to keep my job I have no choice then, do I," responds Tavin as he hangs up the phone. Tavin's phone rings again and he answers it, "Look asshole, are you calling me back to rub it in my face some more?" argues Tavin. "Ah, no sir, your wife is on line two." surprisingly slowly responds Christal. "Thank you Ms. MacKenley." replies Tavin.

Captain Briar MacKenzie knocks on Tavin's office door. "Come on in Captain, what brings you here?" asks Tavin. "Well Administrator, I just came in to question one of your girl's and now that I am done I thought I would pop in to see how you are doing getting settled in." replies Briar. "Well, I am getting settled in just fine, thank you. I need you to do something for me Chief?" asks Tavin. "Sure Administrator, whatever you need." replies Briar. "I need you to send out a B.O.L.O. (Be On the Look Out) for Mrs. Sandra MacQuire of DCFS, she has taken a couple of my children from the Children's Home, and she has not yet brought them back." says Tavin. "Who did she take Tavin?" asks Briar. "She has taken Rhobert Rodriguez, and Carla Ashton." replies Tavin. "Do you think she knows?" asks Briar. "I do not know for sure, but I do know that we cannot risk it. If she finds out, then we are through." responds Tavin. "Well Administrator, I believe that I need to also put out an Amber Alert then, and if she is caught we will arrest her for abduction and kidnapping." says Briar. "Sounds good to me Briar." replies Tavin. "You do realize Tavin, that once she is picked up and brought in, the plan is to also add her to the missing persons list?" asks Briar. "Yes that sounds like a very good plan Briar." replies Tavin.

Tavin calls his Secretary, "Yes, Ms. MacKenley, do you have a minute to come into my office?" "Yes sir I will be right there." replies Christal as she hangs up her phone. Christal steps up to the open door and knocks, "Yes please come on in." states Tavin. "Ms. MacKenley in the next few months, we are going to be getting job applications for the new positions for the Youth Detention Center annex. Here is a list of those positions, and their position qualifications. I want you to keep a list of all the applications received, and their status. If they do not meet the position qualifications for the position, then send a not considered thank you letter and add them to the list as a no hire. Those that are received that meet the position qualifications, I want to see them, and I will give them back so that you can schedule an interview time for them to come in and see me. Before you give the qualified ones to me to review, I want you to run a back ground check on them first. I want you to keep track of them on the list. I want to know who they are, position applied, do they qualify, if no date thank you sent, if yes status of back ground check, and date of scheduled interview. Understand that you may receive applications in person, or in the mail. The applications received in person, take them, and tell the person we will get back to them we are just reviewing right now. Do you have any questions Ms. MacKenley?" asks Tavin. "No sir, I got it." replies Christal. "Good, thank you Ms. MacKenley." responds Tavin. "Oh yes Ms. MacKenley, any application that comes in claiming to be an ex-Navy Seal give it directly to me." orders Tavin. "Yes sir will do." replies Christal.

Detective MacKlain knocks on Captain MacKenzie's Office door. "Come in detective, what do you got?" asks Briar. "Well sir, we think we may have found Mr. Bud Dyer's car sir." replies Detective MacKlain. "What do you mean you think you may have?" asks Briar. "Well sir, we found heavy rubber tire tracks, a busted guard rail at mile marker five of the scenic route outside of town, burnt debris all the way down into the lake, and a burnt mangled license plate that was found. We ran the plate and it was Mr. Dyer's. I called in the divers they did not find a body in or around the car in the lake. Also, a body was not found among the wreckage debris on the trip down to the lake. The divers did find a crowbar believed to be the possible murder weapon. Since it was in the fire, and later found in the lake we are unable to run a DNA test on it." responds Detective MacKlain. "OK thank you detective." says Briar.

Briar calls his brother Dan, "Yea brother it is me Briar." states Briar. "Yes Chief, what do you need?" asks Dan. "Well brother, we have located Mr. Bud Dyer's car. It appears to have been set on fire and driven off the cliff on the scenic route just outside of town. A license plate was recovered, indicating that it was Mr. Bud Dyer's car. Divers did not recover a body; nor was there a body recovered from the cliff. Divers recovered a crowbar believed to be the murder weapon; but since it was involved in the fire and later recovered from the car in lake we are unable to run a DNA test. Heavy tire tracks perpendicular to the road at the crashed guard rail on the scenic route, with no body; leads us to believe that the body is located at another unknown crime scene the suspect was just getting rid of the car and the murder weapon. So until a body is found I will keep the B.O.L.O. open. I am also sending Cadaver Dogs to his place of residence to search the premises for a body. Also, just to let you know, I have put out an Amber Alert for his daughter, Sarah Dyer. She is nowhere to be found, she was staying at the Children's Home; but she is no longer at the Children's Home either. She disappeared a day before Mr. Dyer came up missing. I believe the two missing people cases are related. No, we don't have any suspects as of yet right now. Then again, without any of the bodies we do not have a case either." states Briar. "Good work Chief, keep me informed if anything new comes up." responds Dan. "I sure will Dan, take care." says Briar as he hangs up the phone.

CHAPTER NINE

Mr. Rodger Boehm an ex-Navy Seal arrives at the Belle Haute Children's Home and parks his vehicle. He gets out of his vehicle and walks the sidewalk to the front entrance in the alcove. He presses the talk button on the speaker box. "Yes, may I help you?" asks Christal. "Yes Ma'am I am Mr. Rodger Boehm I was referred here to apply for the Security Leader Supervisor position." says Rodger. "I will be right there sir." replies Christal. Christal unlocks the door to let Rodger in, and then she locks the door as he steps in. When she is done locking the door, Rodger extends his hand to her, "I am Rodger Boehm, Senator MacKenzie referred me here to apply for the Security Leader Supervisor position." states Rodger. "OK sir, let me go get you an application to fill out." says Christal as she goes back to her office to get an application for Rodger. "Here you are sir. Just fill this out and bring it in to me when you are finished filling it out." states Christal as she hands Rodger an application. "May I ask, are you the ex-Navy Seal that we are expecting?" asks Christal. "Yes Ma'am that is me, I am the one." says Rodger. "OK, thank you." replies Christal. Christal goes back to her office, goes up to the Headmaster's Office door, and knocks, "Yes Ms. MacKenley?" asks Tavin. "Yes sir, a Mr. Rodger Boehm the ex-Navy Seal is here to fill out an application. You had told me you wanted to see him should he show up." replies Christal. "Yes, of course send him in, please." directs Tavin. Christal brings Rodger to the door, "Sir, Mr. Rodger Boehm." states Christal. "Yes thank you Ms. MacKenley." responds Tavin. Tavin gets up and extends a hand out to Rodger, "Hello Mr. Boehm, please come in take a seat at the table and finish filling out your application while we speak." directs Tavin. "Thank you sir." says Rodger, as he shakes Tavin's hand and sits down. "So Mr. Boehm, how long were you a Navy Seal?" asks Tavin, remaining behind Rodger. "Well sir, I was a Navy Seal for twenty five years." replies Rodger. Making sure that his Secretary is not watching, Tavin quickly wraps his forearm around Rodger's neck and snaps Rodger's neck with his free arm, lets his limp body rest against the conference table. Tavin then closes and locks his office door. Tavin then sits down at his desk and calls Torey, "Yes hello Mr. Reid, I need you to grab a shovel, an extra large black plastic bag and your wheel barrel, come over here into the backyard and dig a four foot long, five foot deep hole. Then bring your wheel barrel and plastic bag into my office, gift wrap the package then wheel the package out into the backyard and burry it in the hole that you dug. I need this pronto." directs Tavin. "Yes sir, right away." replies Torey. Tavin then steps out into Ms. MacKenley's office and he goes up to Ms. MacKenley, "Ms. MacKenley, could you please run into town to the bakery and pickup the cake that I ordered, for me please?" "Yes sir, sure I will." replies Christal. Tavin gives Christal the money that she would need to pay for the cake. As soon as Christal leaves, Tavin goes back into his office, shuts the door, and calls the Bakery and orders a cake for Christal to pick up.

Christal drives into the once quiet little town of Pays des, to the Pays des Bakery; she parks her car and gets out. As Christal enters the bakery, her friend Mrs. Brenda Wilson asks, "Hey girl just what the hell is going on out there? We have many people missing, and several Amber Alerts. Mr. Dyer's car found in the lake, but they have not found his body." "Well Brenda, although that is all true, I have no idea what is going on; it is all news to me. Awfully sad, if you ask me; and scary too." says Christal. "So Christal, how do you like your new boss?" asks Brenda smiling. Christal rolls her eyes, "He is an arrogant pompous ass like his brother." replies Christal. "Now Christal, you know that you like having a new ass to kiss." laughingly teases Brenda. Christal waves her middle finger at Brenda, moving her lips without speaking as if to say, "Fuck you." Brenda starts to laugh, causing Christal to laugh with her. Teasing Christal laughingly tells Brenda, "Just give me the cake bitch." "Don't get you panties in a wad Hooker." laughingly replies Brenda. As

Brenda boxes up the cake, trying to keep a straight face, she asks Christal, "So tell me, have you slept with him yet?" "No!" surprisingly responds Christal. "Are you going to?" asks Brenda. "That's none of your damned business girl friend." replies Christal. "I know you want too." states Brenda. "I hate him. I would not touch him with a ten foot pole." replies Christal. "Really, that bad huh?" asks Brenda. "You can have him though." laughs Christal. "I do not want your sloppy seconds." laughs Brenda as she hands Christal the boxed cake. Christal hands the money for the cake over to Brenda. Brenda rings up the sale on the register, and hands Christal the change and tells Christal, "Have a good day girl friend. Do something I would." says Brenda. "You to, and do not worry, if I do I will name it after you." laughingly replies Christal as she leaves.

After digging the hole, Torey takes the wheel barrel and plastic bag to Tavin's office. He knocks on the door and Tavin unlocks and cracks the door open, "Did anyone see you, is my Secretary gone?" asks Tavin. "No one saw me, and your Secretary is gone." replies Torey. Tavin opens the door to his office to let Torey in, and then Tavin closes and locks the door behind Torey. Together Tavin and Torey quickly work to put Mr. Boehm's lifeless corps in the plastic bag. After sealing the plastic bag, they place the bag into the wheel barrel. Tavin unlocks his office door and steps outside of his office to make sure that the coast is clear. Satisfied that the coast is clear, Tavin tells Torey, "Go ahead and get the body in the bag out of my office." He then hands Torey the keys to Mr. Boehm's car and Mr. Boehm's home address telling Torey, "When you are finished burring the body, drive Mr. Boehm's car back to his home address. Also, when you are handling Mr. Boehm's car make sure that you wear gloves. When you get the car to Mr. Boehm's home address, make sure the coast is clear, and that no one see's you leaving it there. Drive the car around the block a couple times if necessary." "Yes sir, will do." replies Torey.

Christal returns to Belle Haute Children's Home and parks her vehicle in the parking lot. She grabs the cake and gets out of her vehicle and walks the sidewalk to the front entrance in the alcove. She unlocks the door steps inside and locks the door back up. She takes the cake into her office and steps up to the Headmaster's Office door and says, "Here is your cake sir." "Thank you Ms. MacKenley, just set it on the table please." replies Tavin. Christal places the cake on the table and returns to her office.

Mr. David McIntire a certified construction Project Manager arrives at the Belle Haute Children's Home and parks his vehicle in the parking lot. He grabs his file folder gets out of his vehicle and walks the sidewalk to the front entrance in the alcove. He makes notice that there is not a security camera trained on the front entrance. He presses the talk button on the speaker box. "Yes, may I help you?" asks Christal. "Yes Ma'am my name is Mr. David McIntire, I am here to speak with the Headmaster Mr. MacKenzie." replies David. "I will be right there sir." says

Christal. Christal unlocks the door to let David in, and then she locks the door as he steps in. When she is done locking the door, David extends his hand to her, "I am David McIntire a certified construction Project Manager here to speak with the Headmaster Mr. MacKenzie." says David. "Yes sir, I am his Secretary. Follow me please and I will take you right to him." replies Christal as she shakes his hand. They walk into Christal's Office, and she goes up to the Headmaster's doorway and knocks on the door. "Yes Ms. MacKenley may I help you?" asks Tavin. "Yes sir, Mr. David McIntire a certified construction Project Manager is here to see you." replies Christal. "Yes, yes of course send him in." states Tavin.

Mr. David McIntire steps into the Tavin's office, Tavin gets up and walks up to him to shake his hand, "Please come in Mr. McIntire have a seat, can I get you a cup of coffee?" asks Tavin as they shake hands. "No thank you." responds David as they both sit down. "As your Secretary said, I am Mr. David McIntire a certified construction Project Manager. I am also bonded. I can guarantee you that I will expertly manage your construction project through to completion with a goal to complete your project on the time we estimate. As long as you understand that I am not in control of unforeseen anomalies that can tie up and prolong the estimated completion time. I will coordinate every aspect of the construction project and work within your designated budget. I will manage all subcontractor bidding, material procurement; ensuring quality control and safety standards. I will work to resolve any issues that could come up in the construction process. I will oversee any and all training of personnel on any new system or equipment operation. I will also provide you with status reports, you just tell me when you want them and how often. Does any of this meet with your approval?" asks David. "Yes sir it does. So what do we do now?" asks Tavin. David takes out a form from his file folder, "OK then, here is what I will do. First I need you to sign this temporary agreement for me. What this form does is it authorizes me to get copies of any building drafting plans you may have already have prepared. If you do not have any drafting plans already drawn up, it authorizes me to work with you to get a set of drafting plans drawn up. With a set of completed drafting plans, I can then write up a contract for you and me to sign. The contract details every aspect of the construction project; the pre-construction, during construction, and post-construction process. The contract will separately estimate time and completion of every aspect on the entire construction project; providing a target project completion date for your project. As I said earlier, unforeseen anomalies can prolong the target project completion date; the contract will contain some possible anomalies, but it is not inclusive barring unforeseen weather or environmental anomalies to name a few. Basically this temporary contract authorizes me to charge your budget for drafting plans, zoning, and permits required to prepare and estimate project cost needed for the contract. Once the temporary contract, as well as the permanent contract is signed you cannot break the contract and hire another Project Manager or contractor without first obtaining proper court order." states David. "Very well, I understand. Where do I sign?" asks Tavin. David shows Tavin where to sign, "Yes sir, just sign right by this "X." "Mr. MacKenzie, do you have drafting plans for your construction project?" asks David. "Yes, Mr. McIntire. They are right here I have a copy already made up for you. Let me get them for you." replies Tavin. Tavin signs the form for David, then gets up to retrieve the drafting plans for David. Tavin hands the plans to David and reaches into his drawer and hands David a key, "I believe that you will also need this to Mr. McIntire. This key is a "master" key to the entire complex; it will unlock any door for you. I will need you to return this key as soon as you are finished with this construction project." states Tavin. "OK thank you, I will make sure that you get this key back when our project is done here Mr. MacKenzie." says David. "Mr. McIntire would you like a tour of the area picked out for the project?" asks Tavin. "Yes sir that would be a good idea." replies David. They stand up to leave, "Right this way, follow me." states Tavin.

Tavin takes David out into the backyard and points out the brick wall where the annex will go. "The Youth Detention Center annex will go here, and the new hallway to the annex will start here at the Girl's Dormitory exit door and alcove and run along the length of the Girl's Dormitory to the new annex. Think of it this way, the new hall way into the new annex will be "T" shaped.

The top of the "T" starts here at the Girl's Dormitory exit door and alcove, all the way pasted this brick wall, running the length of the new annex. The base of the "T" hallway will run along this brick wall here with exit doors locked on both sides with alcoves one for the Boy's and one for Girl's Dormitories of the new annex. The difference between the new annex exit doors and the current Children's Home dormitory exit doors; is the Children's Home exit doors are only locked on the outside. The new hallway that starts at and runs the length of the Children's Home Girl's Dormitory; will be locked on both sides and barred. The current exit door and alcove for the Children's Home Girl's Dormitory will be pushed out from where it is now to make room to the new hallway; because we cannot have entrance and exit to the new annex outside in the backyard. This hallway into the new annex will not be empty. The walls on both sides of the hall will be lined with small lockers stacked on top of each other approximately five high; similar to those at an airport each with their own key. There will also be a dividing wall in the center of the hallway. Male juveniles will be admitted on one side, and female juveniles will be admitted on the other side. They will put their street clothes in a locker, take the key and put a name tag on it and turn it over to the security guard who will keep it under lock and key until they are ready to be released. The other part of the "T" hallway that runs the length of the new annex will be a hallway for the new offices being built for the new annex; an office for Security Personnel, an office for a Nurse, and a general use office. The general use office will be for meetings, training, interviews, and DCFS personnel. Well Mr. McIntire, if you don't mind this will end our area tour, I will take you back inside so that you can gather your files." states Tavin. "Not a problem Mr. MacKenzie, thank you for the tour. I will take my files and blue prints home and get started on our permanent contract. All I ask is that you give me 24 hours to get back to you on the permanent contract?" asks David as they walk towards the alcove for the Boy's Dormitory. "Sure Mr. McIntire, not a problem. Let me know if you need more time." responds Tavin as he reaches into his pocket for the key. As David stands waiting for Tavin to unlock the exit door, he takes notice of the newly turned earth against the brick wall between the exit door alcoves to the Boy's and the Girl's Dormitories; where Torey has buried the ex-Navy Seal Mr. Boehm, but David does not know that yet. He also takes notice of minute imprints of a small tire surrounded by foot prints leading up to the pile of newly turned earth. They go inside walking the hall back to the Headmaster's Office. On the way, David senses the faint smell of death as they pass the door labeled, "STORAGE ONLY NOT AN EXIT." As they enter the Headmaster's Office to get David's files and blue prints, Tavin reminds David, "Mr. McIntire, I am sure you know, and since we did not mention it, I feel I should make mention now. The entire construction project needs to have heavy and high makeshift barriers to prevent unwanted entrance into the construction area. Should one of my children try to escape, or run away." states Tavin. "Yes Mr. MacKenzie of course. I will make sure of it." replies David as he starts to leave the Headmaster's Office. "Also, Mr. McIntire, your master key will let you out." reminds Tavin. "Yes sir of course." replies David as he heads out to leave the Children's Home.

CHAPTER TEN

David MacQuire calls his sister Sandra MacQuire; there is no answer after trying to call her home telephone number. So he calls her cell phone number and she answers it, "Hey sis how are you doing? Are you OK?" asks David. "No David, I am not OK!" replies Sandra. "What is wrong sis?" asks David. "Oh David you really got to help me, I have nowhere else to turn, nowhere else to go. The local police have issued a warrant for my arrest, they have put out a B.O.L.O. on me, and they have issued Amber Alert's for both of the two children that are with me. I am absolutely positive that if they were to find us right now; that they would definitely kill us." nervously replies Sandra. "Alright sis calm down. Where are you at right now?" reassuringly asks David. "We are at a cabin down by the lake in the state park." replies Sandra. "I will be right there sis, wait till I get there." responds David.

David drives around the state park looking for Sandra's parked car by one of the many cabins. He finally spots her car at a cabin down by the lake. David slows down when he gets close to make sure that no one else is around. Pleased that no one else is around or watching him he pulls his car up next to Sandra's car and cautiously gets out of his car. He goes up to the cabin door and lightly knocks saying, "Sis it is me David." Sandra opens the door for David, David steps inside closing the door behind him. "OK sis here is what we are going to do. We are going to swap cars because they are not looking for my car. You are then going to take yourself and the children to a safe house that I have arranged for you out of state in Indiana," states David. "Thank you so much David, I am so very scared." replies Sandra. "Oh sis I am so sorry do not be scared, do not worry or blame yourself. This is not your fault you have done nothing wrong. They are the ones who are breaking the law not you." reassures David. "I know David, but this is how they normally operate when they discover that someone has found them out." says Sandra. "Well sis we both have suspected that they were getting away with all of this child abuse for a very long time. We never once suspected that it would also involve murder. So now that we are positive that murder is involved then it is time that I step in and stop them once and for all." responds David. "I hope I am doing the right thing." says Sandra. "Do not worry sis you are doing the right thing." reassures David.

"OK sis you said that you had something for me. What do you have for me?" inquires David. "Here are the little bone fragments that look like a little child's finger, and here is the key to the cellar door that is located in solitary." states Sandra as she gives the bone fragments and cellar key to David. "What do you mean by solitary; where is this solitary?" asks David. "Well David, the children that they feel have misbehaved are sometimes beaten and then taken to the basement and shackled and chained to the wall in the nude without food and water. Rhobert was down there before I got there, and there is no telling how long they would have left him there without food and water." says Sandra. "So you mean to tell me that the children at the Children's Home are sometimes locked up in the basement without food and water and they call it solitary confinement?" asks David. Rhobert and Carla both respond by shaking their heads, "Yes sir they do." "Carla and Rhobert I am so very sorry to hear that you had to endure such abuse." responds David. "So Carla, Rhobert can you tell me how to get to this solitary at the Children's Home?" asks David. "Yes sir it is in the basement. You go to the door that is labeled "STORAGE ONLY NOT AN EXIT" they always keep that door locked." says Carla. "The cellar door is at the bottom of the steps that lead into the basement and it is on your right. It is a small square door." says Rhobert. "While Rhobert was in solitary he found the key to the cellar door still in the key lock and he was able to take it. Rhobert got himself free from the shackles and chains, and used the key to open the cellar door. He went inside the cellar area and he saw a rotting body of a little girl, and then on the far back wall of the cellar area there is a small steel oven looking box. Rhobert opened it up and found the finger bones in it." says Sandra.

"Also in the hallway in between the Girl's and the Boy's Dormitories there are two interview rooms. Inside both rooms there is a bare mattress on the floor. The walls of these rooms have foam all over the walls from the floor to the ceiling." says Rhobert. "Yea that is where they take children to sexually abuse them." adds Carla. "How do you know this, have you ever been taken there?" asks David. "No sir I have never been taken there, but other girls who have been taken there told me about it." says Carla. "Yea they also take boys there too." adds Rhobert. "Do you know who takes the children there?" asks David. "Yes sir the men on the staff, the Headmaster, the Assistant Headmaster, the House Father, the Maintenance guy, the police, and the Senator." says Carla. "Also, the Priest takes boys in there too." replies Rhobert.

"Carla watched them bury her sister after her sister had run away from the Children's Home. She went to a nearby neighbor's house for help. The neighbor went to the police to tell them what the sister had claimed was going on at the Children's Home. So that word would not get out about them they killed both the neighbor and the sister. They then buried them both by the tree in the backyard of the Children's Home." says Sandra. "Carla can you tell me who at the Children's Home killed your sister and that neighbor?" asks David. "Yes sir, it was the House Father Mr. Anderson and the Maintenance Grounds Technician Mr. Reid." replies Carla. "Thank you for letting me know this Carla. I am so very sorry that they did that Carla." says David.

"OK sis here are the keys to my car, give me yours." says David as they trade car keys. "Alright, sis now I want you to get the kids, get in the car and drive to this address in Indiana. Here are the keys to the house at that address." states David as he hands Sandra the directions and the house keys. "Once you get there I want you to stay there until I call you. You will be safe there. Do not come back for any reason unless I call you, understand?" demands David. "OK let's get ready, I will follow you out to the highway to make sure you are OK and that you are not followed." says David. Sandra, Carla, and Rhobert get into David's car. David gets into Sandra's car waiting for Sandra to leave. Sandra pulls out onto the road, and David pulls out behind her following her. With David close behind, Sandra leaves the State Park and gets on the main road that leads to the Highway. They both make it to the Highway heading towards the Indiana boarder. David follows Sandra to the Indiana boarder making sure Sandra and the kids are safe, and then he turns the car around heading back to town. He takes the Airport exit off the Highway and then parks Sandra's car in the Long Term parking lot. David then walks down to the Arrival Terminal, taking the escalator down to the Baggage Area. He then walks passed the baggage carousels and over to the Rental Car desk. He completes the paperwork, shows his driver's license to the clerk and then hands the clerk his credit card to rent a car. The clerk gives him his credit card back and the keys to the rental car. The clerk then calls for the car to be brought to David. When the car arrives outside David is notified. He walks outside to where the rental car sits running waiting for him, he gets into the rental car and drives over to the Long Term parking lot where he parked Sandra's car. He gets his files and Children's Home blue prints from out of her car, puts them into his rental car, and then he heads back home.

Once he gets home, as he drives by his sister's house he notices a car staked out on the street watching her house. He is also positive that they have her telephone bugged too. He gets out his cell phone and calls his sister's home telephone number. He lets the phone ring till the message system turns on and leaves a message, "Yea sis, it's me David. I just wanted to let you that I did not find anything, so I am going back home to Virginia. I will call you when I get home. Take care, love you, bye." David knows that they know that his sister has a brother who is in the FBI. So he left the message to throw them off. Once David gets home, he gets himself a drink from the refrigerator, turns the TV on, then settles down to study the Children's Home blue prints. Looking over the blue prints David finds the two Interview Rooms that Rhobert and Carla said that children were being sexually abused in; however, he cannot find the basement where solitary is located. The door and the basement are not included on these blue prints. David counts the pages and page numbers from the title box on the blue prints that he has copies of, and he discovers that several pages are missing from the blue prints he was given. The missing prints must definitely be the prints of solitary and the cellar area in the basement.

A UPS carrier carries a package up to the door and knocks, Elizabeth answers the door. "Is Mrs. Elizabeth MacKenzie home?" asks the UPS man. "That is me." says Elizabeth. "Ma'am please sign here for me." says the UPS man as he hands over a pen and clipboard to Elizabeth. She signs her name and hands back the pen and clipboard. The UPS man gives Elizabeth a letter sized package and leaves. As she is taking her package towards the kitchen, Dan asks, "Who was that at the door hun?" "It was for me, a UPS package I had to sign for it." says Elizabeth continuing towards the kitchen. Once in the kitchen she opens the package and dumps the contents onto the counter. Six pictures fall out onto the counter; she looks inside the package to make sure that there was nothing else in it. The package is empty; it only contained the six pictures and that is all it contained. She picks up the six pictures and looks at them. Suddenly shocked, stunned, and frozen in place the pictures fall from her shaking hands back onto the counter. Thousands of emotions begin racing through her head. She screams crying, "**NO! NO! NO! AAAHhh!!!**" Dan comes running into the kitchen, asking "Hun, are you OK?" "**GET AWAY FROM ME YOU BASTARD! DON'T EVEN TOUCH ME YOU SON OF A BITCH!**," cries while screaming. "What did I do?" asks Dan. Elizabeth picks up the pictures with her shaking hands and throws them at Dan, and begins to pound her fists with some of the pictures still in her hand, on Dan's chest. Pictures falling as she pounds her fist, "**HOW COULD YOU! YOU SICK BASTARD! HOW COULD YOU!**" crying screams Elizabeth. Dan pushes her away and picks up some pictures to look at them. He is suddenly shocked to learn they are pictures of him having sex with an unwanting twelve year old. "Oh God, no! Elizabeth these are not me! Do not believe them! Someone is setting me up!" states Dan. "**SHUT UP GET AWAY FROM ME YOU SON OF A BITCH JUST GET AWAY FROM ME!**" screams Elizabeth. Someone knocks on the front door Dan leaves Elizabeth in the kitchen to go answer the door. Dan opens the door to find a couple men in suits both holding up their badges and ID's. "Senator Daniel MacKenzie?" they ask. "Yes, that is me." says Dan. "You are under arrest for eight charges of criminal child sexual abuse. You have the right to remain silent, anything you say can and will be used against you in court. You have the right to an attorney, if you cannot afford one, one will be appointed for you." states one of the men as the other man puts the handcuffs on Dan.

David's blue print attention is suddenly interrupted by a special news report on the TV. Interested David grabs the TV remote and turns up the volume. Christal has the TV in her office on, she immediately runs across the hall to her brother's office, "Bill you got to come see this report on the news it is about Senator MacKenzie." claims Christal. Tavin sees and hears the commotion, gets up and joins Christal and Bill in Christal's office to find out what the commotion is all about. The Janitor Mr. Douglas Quinn while passing Christal's office hears the commotion and he steps in to Christal's office to join in listening to the special news report. "Julie Fox of Pays des KSAP news here with this Special Report. We are live at Senator MacKenzie's home were Senator MacKenzie has just been arrested with eight charges of criminal child sexual abuse with a minor handed down by a recent Grand Jury Indictment. The criminal child sexual abuse with a minor is believed to have occurred at the Pays des Belle Haute Children's Home. The charges stem from pictures of Senator MacKenzie having sex with a minor that were submitted by an anonymous tipster. The Senator with his attorney is being escorted to the police vehicle. Senator what can you tell us about these charges." asks Mrs. Fox. "I am totally innocent of these trumped up charges. I never committed the crime they are accusing me of. I am being set up for a crime that I did not commit. My attorney and I look forward to the opportunity of going to court to prove my innocence." replies Senator MacKenzie as he gets into the police vehicle. "Joining us now is Professor Brian Lawson a Criminologist from the Pays des University. Professor what can you tell us about these charges of criminal child sexual abuse with a minor?" asks Julie Fox. "Well Julie it is not unusual for a single event to carry this many charges. Also Julie each of the eight separate charges is a Class 2 Felony, and if he is convicted he could face twenty five plus years in prison for each count." responds Professor Lawson. "Thank you

Professor. This is Julie Fox of KSAP News we will keep you informed as this event continues to unfold. We now take you back to your regularly scheduled programming." says Julie Fox.

"Oh my God can you believe this?" states Christal. "Alright everyone shows over, get back to work **NOW!!!**" responds Tavin as he goes back to his office shutting the door behind him. "Damn what a tight wad." laughingly replies Christal. Doug cheerfully smiling steps out of Christal's office back to his cleaning cart. He takes his cart to the Janitor Cleaning Locker, puts the cleaning cart away, signs out and leaves the Children's Home.

"Wow Bill looks like someone had it out for the Senator." says Christal. "Yea it is going to get pretty hot around here now too sis." replies Bill. "You really think so brother?" asks Christal. "Yes sis, since they know he committed the crime here at the Children's Home." replies Bill. "What should we do brother?" asks Christal a little worried. "Nothing sis, there just coming to investigate what the Senator did, and that's all." says Bill. "Should we leave and not come back?" asks Christal. "No of course not, if you leave and do not come back, they will just get more suspicious." responds Bill. "If you say so brother." replies Christal. "Yes I say so sis. Come on let's call it a day and go home, I will cook this time." says Bill. "OK your on." replies Christal as they leave.

CHAPTER ELEVEN

David arrives at the Belle Haute Children's Home parking lot, and parks his car in the far end of the parking lot, out of sight as much as possible. Mr. Douglas Quinn, the Janitor walks out of the Children's Home and gets into his car and leaves. David hunches down in his seat to let Doug's car pass behind his so as not to be seen. Several minutes later, Bill and Christal come out walk to their own car's get in and leave together. Once again, David hunches down in his seat to let their cars pass behind his so as not to be seen. David realizes that now he is only waiting for Mr. Mackenzie to leave the Children's Home. After several hours of waiting he gets the impression this wait may be awhile. David sees movement on the lawn of the far opposite end of the Children's Home. It's Torey coming from the Maintenance Garage. Suddenly Torey stops looking toward the Headmaster's car which is still parked in the Headmaster's designated spot in the parking lot. That lets Torey know that the Headmaster is still here at the Children's Home. So Torey turns around and heads back to the Maintenance Garage where he just came from. Another hour goes by and the Headmaster has still not left yet. David sees Torey coming from the Maintenance Garage again. Torey stops, sees Headmaster's car that is still parked in the Headmaster's designated spot in the parking lot. So again Torey turns around and heads back to the Maintenance Garage where he just came from. David begins to curiously wonder what Torey is up to. Apparently Torey is waiting for the same thing that David is waiting for; for the Headmaster to leave for the night. A little while longer Tavin walks out of the Children's Home and gets in his car and leaves. David hunches down in his seat to let Tavin's car pass behind his so as not to be seen.

David watches as Torey comes from the Maintenance Garage, and continues on to the front door in the alcove and lets himself in. After a few more minutes of waiting, David gets out of his car and walks to the front door in the alcove. He unlocks the door steps in, and closes the door behind him and relocks the door. David walks the hallway of the Administration Office's, then turns the corner to the left of the long hallway that leads to the Boy's Dormitory and stops. David takes out a flash light, blinks it on then off looking for the solitary door. He notices that he is just ten paces away from the door he is looking for. Once at the door David can smell the faint smell of death. He gets out the master key that he had been given. He does not know for sure if the key he

116

was given will unlock this particular door. David gives the key a try in this door, the door unlocks and he steps inside closing the door behind him. David remembers that Rhobert had told him that this door is only locked from the outside. Once inside the door he turns on his flash light, finds the light switch, and turns on the lights to solitary. As he turned on the lights, he begins to worry about the lights being on shining through any windows this late at night. Once at the bottom of the steps he notices that there are not any windows in solitary. David also recognizes that the faint smell of death is now even stronger. Since there are no windows in solitary he is not so worried about the lights being on.

David finds the cellar door right where Rhobert told him it was. He gets out the key that Rhobert gave to him to unlock the cellar door. While unlocking the cellar door he notices that the little door is caulked. So he knows that with the door caulked he will have to apply a little more pulling pressure to open the door. David pulls hard and the door opens with a dull pop. David is suddenly aware of why the door was caulked as he is over come by the smell of rotting corpse. He looks inside the cellar door with his flash light and sees the rotting corpse of the little girl Rhobert told him about. Using his cell phone he takes pictures of the corps. While taking the pictures he notices something and he moves in for a closer look. He notices that the corps does not have any teeth; he also knows that forensics will now have to resort to other means for DNA and personal identification of this body. David sees the oven like box where Rhobert said he found the finger bones. So he crawls inside up to the oven like box, and when he gets up to it he realizes that what once may have been a coal furnace is now a small gas fed crematory furnace with retort and hopper. He opens the steel door and pulls out a metal tray on rollers. The inside of the furnace is lined with refractory bricks. There is no smell of gas, so David believes the gas is turned off somewhere else in the building. He uses a pencil to rummage through the ashes on the tray being careful making sure he does not knock any off the tray. He is able to make out a few more bone fragments, but he does not touch them leaving them for the forensics team to find later. Using his cell phone he takes more pictures again. When done he pushes the tray back inside the furnace and closes the steel door. With nothing else catching his intuitive eye, David begins to crawl out of the cellar.

Torey escorts one of the girls from the Girl's Dormitory that he has chosen to the door labeled, "STORAGE ONLY NOT AN EXIT." He takes out his key and unlocking the door he pushes the girl through the door and guides her down the steps of solitary. Torey is curious about finding that the lights are already on, but blows it off on the fact that someone must have forgot and left them on. Once at the bottom of the steps, stunned Torey lets go of the girl. The girl takes off running back up the steps and out of solitary. Torey remains fixated on something he did not expect to find in solitary; David crawling out of the cellar door brushing the dirt off of his clothes. With key in hand getting ready to relock the door, he realizes that he is being watched. Torey starts at David, "Just who the hell are you and what do you think you are doing down here? You do not belong down here." He swings his fist high at David hoping to catch him with a right upper cut, and immediately starts to swing with the left for a shovel hook to the stomach. In a split second David blocks the upper cut swing, and grabs the shovel hook left twisting Torey's left hand quickly twirling behind Torey bringing Torey's left arm behind Torey and up in excruciating pain while slamming him face first into the cement wall. "You know something pal, I was just wondering the same damn thing when I saw you bringing that little girl down here. What were you going to do, rape her, then kill her and put her in the cellar like you did to all of the rest of them?" retorts David not expecting an answer. David quickly puts Torey in handcuffs pushing him into the cubical isle throwing him into the first cubical on the right. The whole time Torey is trying to speak, "Hey wha…hey what are you…" David leaves the handcuffs on Torey and connects all of the shackles to the handcuffs. "Hey what are you doing? You cannot leave me down here. Just who do you think you are?" yells Torey to a nonresponsive David. David opens the closet door over Torey yelling, he finds a couple cleaning rags and some duct tape on a shelf. He grabs the rags and the duct tape, and goes back over to where Torey is in the cubical. With a quick blow to the face he knocks Torey out cold. David grabs Torey as he falls limp and rests him in a sitting position against the back wall of the cubical. He then rolls up one of the rags in a tight ball stuffing it into Torey's mouth and covers Torey's mouth with a couple pieces of long duct tape making sure that he does not cover Torey's nose so that the idiot can breathe.

David breaks the lock off of the cellar door and leaves the cellar door open. The disgusting smell will eventually seep upstairs into the hallway. He then proceeds up the steps to the door that locks only from the outside. David opens the door and steps out. Holding the door open with his foot, he reaches into his pocket and takes out his keys looking for one that is old or that he does not need. Finding one, he jams it into the lock on the outside of the door and then he breaks the key off in the lock in the open position so that the door does not lock when closed. He takes out his handy Gerber knife pulling out the phillips head screw driver part and begins to take off all of the screws from the upper door hinge making it virtually impossible to close the door now. David's motive behind doing this is that he believes that it is time to stop hiding behind the solitary secret.

David moves on back to the Administrative Office's with his master key he unlocks the Headmaster's Secretary Office door letting himself in then shuts and locks the door. He goes into the Headmaster's Office taking out his flash light going over to the credenza opening the top drawer. He puts the little flash light in his mouth holding it with his teeth while using both hands to rifle through the blue prints looking for the two pages that were missing from the ones that he was given. David finds the two pages he takes them rolls them up, shuts the drawer, grabs and turns off his flash light, and leaves the office stopping to lock the door shut. He unlocks the exit door, steps outside and locks the door back. He walks the blue print pages out to his car, unlocks the door puts the prints in his car, and shuts and locks the door back.

David walks over to the Maintenance Garage with no idea what he is looking for, but presumes that someone as bad as Torey must have lots of secrets to find. While looking over some of the stuff on the table, the telephone rings and David picks it up, "Hello." starts David, but is cut off by the caller. "Alright you stupid idiot listen up. Your next target is Mr. David McIntire the Project Manager for the new Regional Youth Detention Center annex. Try not to boggle this one up." states the voice on the telephone. "Well I am afraid you are going to have to do your own dirty work this time dirt bag. I am just a little bit tied up right now; besides you said that I am a stupid idiot. Stupid idiots do not work well with dirt bags." responds David. "Look do not make me come over there, you will not like it if I do!" replies the voice. "Look pal make an appointment with my secretary, I have got to catch up on some sleep right now." states David. "You asked for it, I'm coming down now!" replies the voice. "If you are that stupid, bring it on." responds David as he hangs up the phone on the caller. David walks over to the Maintenance Garage fuse box takes out the main fuse letting it fall to the floor. He then walks over to the garage entrance door. He notices that the entrance door opens into the garage. From where the opening of the door is, David looks into the garage for a safe hiding spot out of sight. He then hides in the new found hiding spot waiting for the caller to show. After about thirty minutes of waiting, David hears and sees the lights of a car pulling up outside. He hears a car door open and close, and he hears footsteps approaching. The door opens and the person reaches out with one hand to turn on the lights, while holding his gun with the other. The lights do not come on immediately so the guy keeps trying to flip the switch. David yells, "FBI! DROP YOUR GUN! PUT YOUR HANDS UP!" The person fires several wild shots in the dark in the direction of David's voice missing David. David fires two shots taking down the person at the door. David runs over to the downed individual, kicking that person's gun away. David gets out and turns on his flash light towards the person lying and bleeding on the floor. He is stunned to learn who the person really is; his name is in bold print on his shirt, he still has his work clothes on. David has just shot the Belle Haute Children's Home Janitor, Mr. Douglas Quinn. David kneels down towards Mr. Quinn who is slowly gasping his last words telling David, "I was going to be Headmaster. I had it all planned…"

CHAPTER TWELVE

Special Agent David MacQuire meets with a team of Agents who are sent to assist him in taking control of the Children's Home. They all meet in the front of Belle Haute Children's Home. David takes them into the Headmaster's Office where they all take a seat at the large conference table. He spreads the Children's Home blue prints out on the table. "OK people I am designating this office as our operating base headquarters. The entire Children's Home and the entire grounds that the Children's Home is on, is now our crime scene. Before we can do anything we need to develop our strategic plan that we all will observe and proceed by. This operation is titled "End The Status Quo." Where the status quo comes from is for the last fifty years the Children's Home staff and several outside senior officials have been on a normal basis abusing these children with all sorts of various forms child abuse to include Aggravated Child Sexual Abuse and Murder of some of the children. Any child who would run away from the Children's Home and go to someone in the outside local community to get away from the abuse here at the Children's Home; would result in murder for both the child and the person that they ran away to. Keep in mind that throughout this entire operation here at the Belle Haute Children's Home, the victims here are definitely the children. Also keep in mind that this is a very delicate operation requiring that everything and everybody operate according to plan. In a nut shell we have three major objectives going on at the same time: (1) apprehending and taking into custody all of the suspects, the entire staff and a few outside senior officials from the local community, Police, and a local Priest are suspects, (2) interviewing all of the children and gathering evidence from them, then releasing them to DCFS custody for care and treatment, and (3) forensically process the entire grounds and all of the Children's Home building."

"Apprehending suspects, first we apprehend all of the staff that is currently still at work here at the Children's Home; those still at work are the House Mother Mrs. Gaven, the House Father Mr. Anderson, and the Maintenance Technician Grounds Keeper Mr. Reid who is currently chained up in the basement. Once apprehended the suspects will be taken to the bus and handcuffed to their seat on the bus. The bus is out of sight by the Maintenance Garage. At the exact same time that the House Mother and House Father are apprehended; the children will need to be moved to the dining room in the kitchen under guarded protection and then they can be individually interviewed there. The remaining staff that has yet to arrive for work: the Assistant Headmaster Mr. MacKenley, the Headmaster's Secretary Ms. MacKenley, the Headmaster Mr. MacKenzie, and the staff Nurse Ms. Anderson; will be apprehended as they arrive. Agents will be standing by inside the front entrance door to take them into custody as they arrive, and then escort them to the bus where they will be handcuffed to their seat on the bus as well. While we are apprehending the staff, several Agents will be sent out to apprehend: the Priest Father Mr. Quinn, the Nun Sister Livingston, the Nun Sister Reeves, Police Officer Mr. Reid, and Chief of Police Captain MacKenzie. Senator MacKenzie is already in custody."

"Our Psychologist Agent Roberts you will lead your team in interviewing the children, gathering any and all evidence to include medical evidence and provide any immediate medical treatment as needed. Once your team is done, you will make arrangements with DCFS to take custody of the children, and you will recommend any outside treatment resources as needed. Upon completion you will report your findings to me. We will be in constant contact with the U.S. Attorney General's Office for pending charges and indictment processing based on the evidence that you gather."

"Agent Drew your forensic team will process the entire Children's Home grounds before coming into the Children's Home building to process the entire building. While outside, once you find anything of forensic significance, you will erect a tent with side walls to prevent leaks to the media. I have also arranged for you to receive a Ground Penetrating Radar (GPR), and several specialized cadaver dogs to help in finding any buried remains. Keep in mind that most all of our buried victims may not have their teeth, since most victims had their teeth removed prior to burial. Be aware that victims without their teeth will require Mitochondrial DNA (mtDNA). Also be aware that in the cellar of the basement there is a small crematory oven that has been used with remains still in it on a tray. I have marked with red on this blue print which is a layout of the grounds and the building of the Children's Home all the current known locations of several bodies. One is buried next to the Children's Home exterior wall in the backyard. Two known subjects are buried next to the tree also in the backyard. One known subject is buried in the far right corner of the backyard. One known subject is buried in the cellar that is located in the basement. You will use this blue print to indicate any additional findings you may incur during your search. Agent Drew it is imperative that you wait to process the grounds of the Children's Home until all of the Staff suspects have been apprehended. We do not want them to notice our operation in progress causing them to drive off and spoil any attempt of apprehension."

"Every suspect that we apprehend will be charged with Child Abuse at this time; with just a couple exceptions, Mr. Anderson the House Father and Mr. Reid the Maintenance Technician will be charged with Murder in the First Degree and Aggravated Child Abuse. I have also compiled a list of possible additional charges that can be included based on the evidence we collect. Keep in mind that this list is not all inclusive. These additional charges include: Neglect, Physical Abuse, Aggravated Child Abuse, Child Sexual Abuse, Aggravated Sexual Battery, Educational Neglect, Medical Neglect, Lewd Acts, Rape, Statutory Rape, Child Molestation, Child Procurement which means to give a child for a favor, Verbal Abuse, Attempted Murder, and Murder. Emotional Abuse and Psychological Abuse to include name calling, ridicule, degradation, excessive criticism, excessive demands, and routine humiliation."

"OK everybody that's it! Let's go to work! First up the Girl's and boy's Dormitories." states Special Agent David MacQuire as he concludes his talk. Agents move out with Special Agent MacQuire as they proceed to the Girl's Dormitory to apprehend Mrs. Gaven. As they enter the Girl's Dormitory, Mrs. Gaven is sitting at her desk in her office. A couple agents stop just outside the dormitory doorway to guard against any possible intruders and to keep any children from leaving. As the rest of the agents continue on to apprehend Mrs. Gaven. Mrs. Gaven stands up to intercept approaching agent's and says, "I am sorry gentlemen, but you are not allowed to be in…" She is abruptly interrupted as an agent moves in and begins to handcuff Mrs. Gaven's hands behind her back. While she is being handcuffed another agent reads her the Miranda rights. Once that Mrs. Gaven is in custody, she is escorted out to the bus and handcuffed to her seat. The two agents at the door begin to line up all the girls to escort them to the dining room in the kitchen. Once that all of the girls are in line and ready, they escort them to the dining room in the kitchen with one agent in the front and one at the rear of the line. With the girls escort to the dining room of the kitchen complete, David and the group of agents move onto the Boy's Dormitory. Once at the Boy's Dormitory two agents stop to guard the entrance door. David and the remaining team of agents move on into the Boy's Dormitory to apprehend Adair. They notice that Adair is getting dressed so they move in quickly to handcuff him. At the same time that the agents are grabbing Adair to handcuff him, a scared and crying naked little girl jumps up out of his bed clutching her clothes running away. Agent Squire a female agent on the team runs after her, she catches up to the naked little girl and helps her to get dressed. "Do not worry dear, we are the FBI, and we are here to arrest that man. Now that he is arrested, he won't ever be able to do that to you again." reassures Agent Squire. Agent Squire escorts the girl to the dining room in the kitchen straight up to Agent Roberts telling him that the little was just raped so that a rape kit is performed on her. David slams Adair face first into the cement wall putting a knee into the middle of his back to hold him against the wall, while at the same time wrenching Adair's arms behind his back and up to handcuff him. While he is being handcuffed another agent reads Adair his Miranda rights. After he is cuffed an agent escorts Adair to the bus and then cuffs him to his seat on the bus. The two agents at the door enter into the Boy's dormitory line up the boys and then they escort the boys to the dining room in the kitchen.

Special Agent David MacQuire takes a few agents with him to the basement to apprehend Torey. David removes the shackles with the chains from behind Torey that were attached to the handcuffs David previously put on Torey. Torey begins to struggle handcuffed with David. David immediately stands Torey up and slams him face first into the cement wall of the cubical and reads Torey his Miranda rights. He shows his badge and I.D. to Torey, "FBI Special Agent MacQuire your days of child abuse, child sexual abuse, and murder are done." Torey still handcuffed, turns his body radically trying to break away from David. David lifts his knee and painfully kicks it into the small of Torey's back slamming Torey back into the cement wall, "Look Mr. Reid, you keep this up I do not have a problem with carrying your lifeless little body to the apprehension bus," states David. David directs one of the agents to also cuff Torey's legs together too before they escort him to the bus. With Torey's legs cuffed, the two agents escort Torey to the bus and handcuff him to his seat on the bus.

David goes back to the Headmaster's Office, while on the way he notices that the two guards at the front entrance door are busy cuffing Bill and Christal and reading them their Miranda rights. Then they escort the two of them to the bus and handcuff them to their seat on the bus. While the two agents are busy with Bill and Christal, with no one at the door, Tavin enters the Children's Home and steps into his office, "Just what the hell do you think you are doing Mr. McIntire?" asks Tavin. With badge and I.D. showing David and one of his agents walk up to Tavin, "FBI Special Agent David MacQuire Mr. MacKenzie. You are under arrest." states David as he handcuffs Tavin. The agent reads Tavin his Miranda rights. "I should have known." says Tavin. "Well sir, just so that you know now, I will not be giving you a contract. As a matter of fact, I like the idea of closing this place down and giving you some time in prison better. You know what? I think you and your brothers could do better job starting a quartet together in prison and sing the jail house blues." responds David. "You son of a bitch!" yells Tavin struggling with the two agents that have him. "Get him out of here." commands David.

David tells Agent Drew, "Mr. Drew your team may now begin processing the Children's Home grounds. I will call the equipment truck in." "Yes sir, I am on it." responds Agent Drew as he begins instructing his team. "Mr. Drew make sure your team is aware that the media is starting to gather outside our crime scene tape." reminds David. Agent Kearney approaches David, "Sir we went to apprehend the Priest Father Quinn and the two Nuns, but they were not there. I was told that they are on their way here to the Children's Home." "Very well Agent Kearney let me know once you have them in custody, and Agent Kearney do not speak to the media as you are leaving or coming back." orders David. "Yes sir, I understand."

replies Agent Kearney. Suddenly there is a commotion outside of the Secretary's Office in the hallway by the entrance door. "This is preposterous. Let go of me you have no right." cries Father Quinn as an agent handcuffs him. David walks up to the cuffed Father Quinn and says, "Father Quinn we have every right. Right now you need give your heart to God, because now your ass is mine." While at the same time other agents are handcuffing the two Nuns. David goes back into the office and asks, "Agent Kearney has anyone gone to get Officer Reid and Captain MacKenzie yet?" asks David. "We are leaving right now sir." says Agent Kearney. "Let me know as soon as you bring them in." orders David. "Yes sir," replies Agent Kearney as he is leaving.

An agent comes up to David and says, "Sir the Pays des Mayor Mr. Ferguson is on line one for you, he is hot sir." "Thank you." says David. David picks up line one, "Yes sir how may I help you?" "Mr. MacQuire just what the hell are you doing to my city? Do you realize that you have got the whole damned community in an uproar?" angrily states Mayor Ferguson. "Mayor Ferguson I am just doing my job. With your permission I would like to come meet you and give you a private briefing before giving the city a press conference concerning my investigation." asks David. "Yes please do, get your ass up here now." responds Mayor Ferguson as he hangs up on David. David orders an agent to have Agent Roberts and Agent Drew to come to his office now. Within minutes Agent Roberts and Agent Drew are at the office. David informs them about the private briefing with the Mayor and pending press conference and he asks them for any updates that he can take with him. Before leaving to go to the Mayor's Office David orders Agent Roberts to call the head of DCFS to meet him at the Mayor's Office. With updates in hand, David has an agent drive him to Mayor Ferguson's Office. As David enters the Mayor's Office he stops at the Mayor's Secretary's desk. David shows his badge and I.D. to the Secretary, "FBI Special Agent Mr. David MacQuire here to see the Mayor." The Mayor's Secretary tells David, "Special Agent MacQuire go on into the Mayor's Office. The Mayor is expecting you." David enters the Mayor's Office, and Mayor Ferguson says, "Take a seat Special Agent MacQuire, I am all ears. Mr. MacQuire, this had better be good."

Chapter Thirteen

Ms. Aileen Anderson, the Nurse for Belle Haute Children's Home, arrives at the crime scene tape outside the Children's Home surrounded by the media that has gathered just outside the crime scene tape. She presents her I.D. to the Agent, and he calls base, "Base the Nurse Ms. Anderson has arrived. Are you ready for me to let her in?" "Yes let her in." replies base. The agent raises the crime scene tape to let Aileen proceed to the Children's Home parking lot. As Aileen parks her car and gets out of her car noticing agents with cadaver dogs and the GPR scanning the front yard of the Children's Home and she is at a complete loss as to what is going on. As she enters the front door in the alcove, she is met inside the door by several agents who proceed to cuff her and read her Miranda rights to her. Just as the agents are getting ready to take her to the bus, Agent Roberts walks up, "Wait I need to ask a few questions." "Yes sir." replies the agents. "Ms. Anderson did you know that the girls from the Girl's

Dormitory were being raped?" asks Agent Roberts. "Yes sir, boys from the Boy's Dormitory are always sneaking over to the Girl's Dormitory." "Did you conduct any test on these rape victims?" asks Agent Roberts. "At first when I was hired yes I did, but these children come and go so quickly from here. So I found it best to just treat them instead, since no one seemed to care. The test never seemed to mount to much anyway, and I found that they just took up too much of my time." responds Aileen. "Ms. Anderson did you know that some of the children were being murdered? Like Ms. Ashton?" asks Agent Roberts. "No I did not know that. That is so sad to hear that she was. It must have happened after she was taken from the Children's Home. I was told that DCFS came and got her." replies Aileen. "What would you say if I was to prove to you that some children have been murdered here?" asks Agent Roberts. "Not here, not by anyone who works here. Everyone who works here are kind hearted, and very professional." replies Aileen. Agent Roberts gives the agents the go ahead to take Aileen to the bus, and then he goes back to the dining room in the kitchen. On his way to the dining room, he sends a text message to David's cell phone, "THE NURSE MS. ANDERSON HAS BEEN APPREHENDED." Once Aileen is handcuffed to her seat on the bus, the bus driver is given the "go ahead" to take everyone on the bus to Booking.

Agent Drew's forensic team of Investigators have just about finished checking the Children's Home front yard when suddenly as they reach the flower beds in front of the evergreen bushes that stretch across the entire front of the Children's Home building, the cadaver dogs and GPR begin going crazy. The Investigators begin erecting white tents from one end of the front of the Children's Home to the other end, with a covered opening in the middle at the front entrance in the alcove. With the tents with side walls erected, Investigators begin running the GPR over the flower beds from one end of the Children's Home to the other end. They pause momentarily to stick a buried body indication flag in the ground at each body that they detect. When done Investigators move on with the GPR, taking it over to the area by the Maintenance Garage. Agent Drew is notified that the work of identifying buried remains in the front yard is complete, buried body flags are in place in the flower beds in front of the building with tents erected. Agent Drew steps outside to count the flags in the flower beds that is in front of the Children's Home. He starts counting buried body indication flags from one end to the other, One, Two, Three, Four, Five, and is taken aback when he is finally done counting at Twenty Six. He sends a text message to David's cell phone, "26 REMAINS FOUND IN FRONT." As Agent Drew is going inside to mark his findings on the blue print in the office, he passes a few of his team members going outside to begin the pain staking process of excavating the flagged remains.

Wearing proper coverall clothing, gloves, and face masks, Investigator's begin using stakes and twine to mark off each of the twenty six individual sites of buried remains. Investigators start at one end of the Children's Home staking sites in the flower beds; continuing all the way to the other end. As it turns out there are thirteen sites on each side of the sidewalk that leads up to the front entrance in the alcove. Also, while marking off the site immediately next to, and to the right hand side of the sidewalk; Investigators find something unusual that was sticking up out of the ground half buried in the dirt. It is a cell phone. An Investigator bags it, and then takes it in to Agent Drew. Agent Drew asks the Investigator, "Whose cell phone is it, and could it just have been dropped in the flower bed?" "We do not know whose cell phone it is sir, and no sir it was not dropped in the flower bed. It was buried sticking up out of the dirt, obviously over looked." replies the Investigator. "You do not know whose cell phone it is, and you did not bother to look? Take it out of the bag." orders Agent Drew. The Investigator takes the cell phone out of the bag. "Now flip it up and tell me what you see," orders Agent Drew. The Investigator complies as ordered. "Well sir there are numerous missed calls from the Children's Home." replies the Investigator. "OK now press the MENU button, then scroll down and select PHONE INFO, then select MY NUMBER, and then write down the cell phone's number so that we can find out whose cell phone it is." orders Agent Drew. The Investigator writes the number down on a piece of paper and gives the paper to Agent Drew. "Thank you, now get back to work." orders Agent Drew. Agent Drew goes to the telephone and makes a call asking for help. He gives the person on the phone the cell phone number asking whose cell phone number is it. After a few minutes on hold, he writes down the name saying thank you before hanging up. He says to himself, "Oh my God." He immediately gets up and goes outside to the site where the cell phone was found. Agent Drew calls one of the Investigator's over to him, and orders him, "Process this site immediately now!" "Yes sir." replies the Investigator. The Investigator kneels down and begins carefully removing the flowers from the flower bed in the marked site. The Investigator places the removed flowers near the line of evergreen bushes. Once all of the flowers are removed from the site, the Investigator takes a trowel and begins to carefully remove the dirt putting removed dirt in large five gallon buckets where the dirt can be later screen sifted for evidence. After removing just a few inches, a blue tarp begins to appear indicating that the buried body was wrapped in the blue tarp. Several more Investigators come over to help carefully remove all of the dirt from around the blue tarp. After all of the dirt around the blue tarp with the body has been carefully removed, the tarp with the body is lifted up and placed on a gurney. Once on the gurney one part of the blue tarp unrolls and falls to the side. A wallet falls unnoticed by the Investigators to the ground. Investigators roll the tarp back up. Agent Drew picks up the wallet and opens it to see whose it is, confirming the same information that he received about the cell phone. Agent Drew sends a text message to David's cell phone, "THE BODY OF MR. BUD DYER FOUND. HE WAS ONE OF THE 26."

Investigators using the GPR and cadaver dogs place buried remains flags over sites found around the Maintenance Garage, and erect white tents with side walls over all of the flagged buried remains sites found. The cadaver dogs begin barking at the entrance door to the Maintenance Garage. Investigators go inside placing a red "X" on the cement floor where remains are found. When completed Investigators begin staking the buried remains sites found around the Maintenance Garage area. Agent Drew walks the area around the Maintenance Garage taking notes counting buried remains flags and their location so that he can mark them on the blue print when he goes back into the Children's Home. He goes into the Maintenance Garage to count and note the buried remains in there. While he is walking around inside logging sites marked with a red "X" by chance he finds a dusty photo album on a shelf. He opens up the photo album and is shocked by what he sees. It appears to be a collection of photographs of bounded and gagged girls that were murdered. Once complete, he goes back inside the Children's Home to the office and sets aside the photo album, with hands shaking he begins to mark on the blue print where the remains around and in the Maintenance Garage were found. When he is done Agent Drew sends another text message to David's cell phone, "18 MORE BODIES FOUND AROUND MAINTENANCE GARAGE, BRINGING THE TOTAL TO 44."

On a hunch, Agent Drew calls for help again. This time he asks for a background check on Mr. Torey

Reid, and provides a fax number. While he is waiting for the fax to come in, he walks over to the coffee pot and makes himself a cup of coffee. He makes his cup of coffee and takes a seat next to the fax machine waiting for the fax to come in. After about fifteen minutes of waiting the fax machine begins to ring and then incoming pages begin to print. When done Agent Drew grabs the pages and begins to read. He is shocked to learn that Mr. Torey Reid has a history of child sexual abuse, rape, and molestation. The first thought that comes to Agent Drew's mind is, Mr. Reid is nothing more than a serial pedophile turned serial killer. Just how in the hell does a man with such a criminal background get a job working at a Children's Home? Agent Drew sends another text message to David's cell phone, "MAINTENANCE TECHNICIAN GROUNDS KEEPER MR. TOREY REID IS A SERIAL PEDOPHILE (CONFIRMED) TURNED SERIAL KILLER."

Agent Drew goes outside to observe the recovery of buried remains process. Investigators are busy sifting dirt on a screen, bagging bones, and evidence from the identified sites. Agent Drew makes sure that the Investigators know that they should move on to help out by the Maintenance Garage when they are done. Satisfied, Agent Drew moves on over to the Maintenance Garage area to assess the recovery process going on there. Investigators are busy sifting dirt on a screen, bagging bones, and evidence from the identified sites. Agent Drew goes inside the garage and is unexpectedly startled by the sudden loud noise as an Investigator begins using a jackhammer on one of the spots on the cement floor marked with an "X." Regaining his composure, Agent Drew takes a look and notices that one of the GPR agents has gone back over the area marked with an "X" and using chalk to mark out where the jackhammer needs to hammer. Once that the Investigator with the jackhammer is done with this one area, he moves on to the next chalked area with the jackhammer. While at the same time other Investigators begin removing chunks of cement placing them in five gallon buckets. Once that the cement chunks are picked up, they begin carefully removing the dirt, putting the dirt in five gallon buckets to be sifted later.

Investigators with the GPR and cadaver dogs, move on to the backyard of the Children's Home. Once again sticking flags in the ground where buried remains are identified. White tents without side walls are erected. Side walls are not required since the backyard is out of sight from the outside. Investigators are petrified as the GPR goes over the spot where the ex-Navy Seal was buried, that he suddenly begins clawing his way out of the ground and stands up brushing off the dirt on his clothes. An Investigator walks up and identifies himself to Mr. Rodger Boehm. Agent Drew arrives after a few minutes and asks, "Mr. Boehm, I am FBI Agent Drew, you understand that we thought you were dead? It is not every day that a detected buried body comes out of the ground on its own without help. If you will come follow me I will take you to our doctor to have her check you out and also I would like to get your statement." "I would like to get my hands on that scrawny little Headmaster bastard." replies Rodger as he follows Agent Drew inside. "What is going on here anyway? Why is the FBI all over the place?" asks Rodger. "We are conducting an investigation." replies Agent Drew. "What are you investigating?" asks Rodger. "Child Sexual Abuse and murder." replies Agent Drew. "Hey look man, I had nothing to do with that, I was attacked during my job interview and buried alive back there." states Rodger. "Mr. Boehm I still need to get your statement. It will help our investigation." responds Agent Drew. "If I help you, will you put in a good word to help me get hired for the job?" chuckling asks Rodger. "Well Mr. Boehm, I believe that job went away when you died back there." laughingly replies Agent Drew.

The Agent at the crime scene tape calls base, "Base Mrs. Diane Kriete from DCFS is here with a bus to pick up the children. Should I let her in?" asks the Agent. "Yes let them in." responds base. Agent Roberts goes to the front entrance to wait for Mrs. Kriete. As Mrs. Kriete approaches the entrance door, Agent Roberts shows her his badge and I.D., "Good afternoon Mrs. Kriete I have twenty seven children for you to pick up. There are sixteen girls, and eleven boys. Here is a list of their names and any medical problems they may currently have with recommended treatments they may need. Just so that you know Mrs. Kriete, since there is not any indoctrination paperwork kept by this Children's Home; I am unable to provide for you how long either one may have been here at the Children's Home. Also, I will need you to sign this document showing that you are receiving into custody these twenty seven children." states Agent Roberts as he hands over all the paperwork to Mrs. Kriete. Mrs. Kriete signs the document that Agent Roberts wanted signed, and hands it back to him. She then puts the remaining documents into her folder. "OK Mrs. Kriete if you will follow me I will take you to the children. Also, Mrs. Kriete I have several Agents standing by they will help escort the children to the bus." states Agent Roberts. "Yes, thank you Agent Roberts." says Mrs. Kriete. They enter the dining room in the kitchen where all the children are, Agent Roberts addresses them, "OK children, this is Mrs. Kriete of the Department of Children's Family Services (DCFS). She will be taking you all to a better facility by bus. The bus is outside waiting for you. I want to personally thank each of you for all the help, kindness, and patience you gave the FBI today. Also as you leave please accept my gift to you. I am giving each of you this FBI handbag, with a FBI hat, and FBI pen inside. Once again it was great to get to know you for this short time. You all were good, and you helped us a lot. I want to wish you all the best. Thank you." says Agent Roberts. "OK children once you get your bag from the Agents by the door you will get in line and follow these kind Agents to the bus outside." instructs Mrs. Kriete. The children all start to get up and go over to get a FBI handbag then line up at the door. A couple Agents begin walking out into the hall to take the children to the bus. Mrs. Kriete walks up to Agent Roberts to shake his hand and say, "Thank you very much Agent Roberts. Good luck with your investigation." "Thank you Mrs. Kriete." replies Agent Roberts. After the children are gone Agent Roberts sends a text message to David's cell phone, "CHILDREN ARE GONE PICKED UP BY BUS BY DCFS. MRS. KRIETE OF DCFS SIGNED FOR THEIR CUSTODY."

After Agent Drew is done getting a statement from Mr. Boehm, he lets him go. After Mr. Boehm leaves, Agent Drew goes back out to the back yard to count and record body remains flags and locations. He counts fifteen flags and records their location. When done counting and recording, Agent Drew goes back to the office to mark his findings on the blue print. While he proceeds back into the Children's Home, Investigators are busy staking the new sites, getting ready to start excavating them. After Agent drew is done marking the blue print, he sends a text message to David's cell phone, "15 BODIES FOUND IN BACKYARD BRINGING TOTAL TO 59."

Finished in the backyard, Investigators take the GPR and cadaver dogs into the Children's Home checking every room and hallway. When done checking every room and hallway, an Investigator reports to Agent Drew that nothing was found in any room or hallway and they are now going to proceed to the basement. Before that they go into the basement Investigators bring a ventilation generator to the front entrance to the Children's Home and run the air supply tube and air exhaust tube down into the basement. Wearing masks they begin to carefully carry the GPR down into the basement and begin searching the basement cement floor for buried remains. Using chalk they mark an outline where the jackhammer needs to hammer. They chalk off four remains found under the cement floor in four of the cubicles, one in each of the four. Once done, they carefully carry the GPR back up out of the basement, and the Investigators retire the cadaver dogs and the GPR. Investigators being done in the backyard, they now move down into the basement wearing proper gear and face masks. A couple Investigators carefully carry the jackhammer down into the basement. A couple more Investigators climb into the cellar and begin the pain staking process of excavating the cellar. Several more Investigators are standing by the cellar door to take the buckets of dirt from the two inside the cellar, handing them empty buckets. They use plastic sheets to individually put uncovered buried remains on so that Investigators can easily pass them through the small cellar opening. As they proceed further into the cellar, two more Investigators climb into the cellar area to help pass buckets and plastic sheets. Once the Investigators reach the small crematory oven, the tray of dust and bones is placed on a plastic sheet, and they use a small brush to brush out the oven onto the plastic sheet. As they pass the plastic sheet with the tray along, they are told crematory remains. It is important that these remains remain separate from the other uncovered remains. Investigators will not know a total remains from the basement until mtDNA processes and separates each of the cremated remains.

While Investigators are busy with the jackhammer on the cement floor, an Investigator reports to Agent Drew that four remains were found under the cement floor in the cubical area, and six remains were uncovered in the cellar area. He also reminds Agent Drew that the total number of remains found in the cellar remains unknown and will possibly increase until mtDNA can separate the cremated remains on the tray of the crematory oven. So right now there is ten (plus) in the basement. Agent Drew and the Investigator mark the basement findings on the blue print. When done Agent Drew sends a final message to David's cell phone, "FOUR MORE BODIES FOUND UNDER BASEMENT CEMENT FLOOR IN CUBICAL AREA. SIX BODIES UNCOVERED IN CELLAR AREA. BRINGING TOTAL TO 69, THIS NUMBER WILL INCREASE AFTER CREMATORY REMAINS ARE DNA TESTED."

CHAPTER FOURTEEN

Special Agent David MacQuire begins to address Mayor Ferguson, "Well good or bad, I am conducting an investigation at the Pays des Children's Home to not only get to the truth, but to also stop the murdering and abuse of innocent children. For the last fifty years innocent children have been abused, neglected, sexually abused, raped, and murdered at the hands of most all of the staff of the Children's Home, a local Priest, two of his Nuns, a Police Officer, the Chief of Police, and a Senator. All of them with the ideological mind set of covering up after each other and quieting the abused children right under the community's noses. For example Mayor Ferguson three years ago a little girl, Ms. Sarah Ashton ran away from the Children's Home to get away from the abuse. She ran to Mrs. Darla Ferguson's house, and told her about the abuse that was going on at the Children's Home. Mrs. Ferguson went to the police to turn the Children's Home in for abuse. Not too long afterwards, Mrs. Ferguson and Ms. Ashton turned up missing." states David. "Yes that was my sister Darla. To this day we are still puzzled about where she is or where she may have gone." responds Mayor Ferguson. "Well Mayor Ferguson, your sister and Ms. Ashton were murdered to silence them, and then they were taken to the backyard of the Children's Home and buried there. We have an eye witness of the burial, Sarah's sister Carla watched them unnoticed bury their bodies in the backyard of the Children's Home. My Investigators are in the process of recovering their remains as we speak. Mayor Ferguson I am deeply sorry for your loss, and I promise you now that the ones who were involved will be brought to justice." states David. "Oh my God! That was my sister! Those bastards!" replies Mayor Ferguson with tears beginning to swell. "Mayor Ferguson if I may. The FBI has not come to the Pays des community to wreak havoc and devastation. We are here to help the community uncover the truth, stop the sadistic murder and abuse of innocent children, and to help bring closure to many families. The FBI has every intention of apprehending each and every person involved and making sure that they are stiffly dealt with and appropriately prosecuted. That is to include respected local senior officials of the community that are involved. Also, Mayor Ferguson, when we conclude here I would like to hold a press conference." states David. The Mayer pages his Secretary, "Alice can you contact the media and schedule a press conference? Let them know that it will be within the hour," requests the Mayor. "Yes sir, right away sir." replies Alice.

"Mayor Ferguson we have apprehended everyone involved, including Senator MacKenzie. I am sure you are aware of his involvement?" asks David. "Yes, it is all over the news." replies Mayor Ferguson. "With everyone now apprehended, my FBI team of Agents are focusing their efforts now on recovering buried remains at the Children's Home. While at the same time interviewing the children, assessing their medical needs and any immediate treatment they may need. I have just been notified that my team has currently recovered twenty six remains in the front yard of the Children's Home, and one of them recovered was Mr. Bud Dyer. We believe that his death was staged so that the Senator could place his brother in charge of the Children's Home." states David. "I've been following his disappearance on the news." replies Mayor Ferguson. "Well Mayor that is what they wanted everyone to believe. First they murdered and buried him, and then they had to get rid of his car." states David. "My God these people are evil they will stop at nothing." replies Mayor Ferguson. "That is pretty much their *Status Quo* or modus operandi Mayor Ferguson." states David. "I heard his daughter was missing too. I just presumed he left town taking his daughter with him." replies Mayor Ferguson. "Like I said Mayor that is exactly what they wanted everyone to believe. Truth be told, the Children's Home had a serial pedophile turned serial killer working for them. He killed the daughter, and then to keep the father from finding out what he had done he had to kill the father. This played right into the Senator's hands for being able to place his brother in charge of the Children's Home. Also Mayor Ferguson I have just been notified that the death toll at the Children's Home has increased, eighteen more bodies have been found bringing the death toll now to forty four." states David. "Oh my God, I had no idea this has been going on over there for so long right under our noses." replies Mayor Ferguson. "Absolutely Mayor, and that is exactly how they liked it, no one knows." states David.

"Mayor Ferguson, did you know that the Children's Home has a small crematory oven that they have been illegally operating without a license?" asks David. "No I never knew about that." replies Mayor Ferguson. The Mayor pages his Secretary, "Alice, get a hold of the Zoning Officer, and the City Manager; find out if we have anything on a crematory at the Children's Home?" asks Mayor Ferguson. "Yes sir, right away sir." says Alice. "Mayor, I just got word that Mrs. Diane Kriete of DCFS has taken custody of all the children she is taking them to safety. Also, Mayor another fifteen bodies have been found in the backyard of the Children's Home bringing the death toll now to fifty nine. Your sister was one of them. I am so very sorry Mayor Ferguson." states David. The Mayor's Secretary pages, "Mayor Ferguson the City Manager Mr. Regan is here to see you." "OK please send him in Alice." replies the Mayor. The City Manager comes into the Mayor's Office, "Mr. Regan this is FBI Special

Agent Mr. MacQuire." states Mayor Ferguson as they both shake hands. "What do you got for me Mr. Regan?" asks the Mayor. "Well sir, the Children's Home is within the Zoning parameters for having a crematory; however, they are required by regulation to submit a request and be approved to operate within the Zone. State law also requires that they apply for and be approved for a Crematory License, and a Crematory Permit; the crematory device is also required to have an Operating Permit. In addition to the State requirements, the Environmental Protection Agency (EPA) requires that they carry an EPA License and Permit. Any operator of the crematory device is required to be Board Certified through the State; as well As, Certified by the EPA. The State also requires that an Annual Report be on file as well. The Annual Report is a yearly record of crematory operation breaking down each individual cremation, charge for each individual cremation; as well as, any operating cost. Each individual cremation on the report also includes Operator name and License number. All License and Permit numbers are to be included in the report as well. With that said, as of right now we hold no record of any License or Permit, nor are there any Annual Reports on file. We also have no record of any Board Certified Operators. Nor do we have a Device Operating Permit on file. We do not know if they have what EPA requires, but I would venture to say they do not since they do not meet State requirements." concludes Mr. Regan. "Thank you Mr. Regan, very good job." replies the Mayor, as Mr. Regan gets up to leave. "Yes thank you Mr. Regan." replies David. "Mayor Ferguson, I have just been notified that ten more bodies have been found, bringing the death toll now to sixty nine. That total may slightly increase later on after DNA testing of crematory remains is concluded," states David. "Mayor Ferguson, just a reminder, your press conference is ready when you are." pages Alice. "Thank you Alice." replies the Mayor.

"Special Agent MacQuire, if you do not mind. Let me contact the Governor, before our press conference. Your welcome to stay if you like." states Mayor Ferguson. "Alice, please contact the Governor's Office for me. Let them know it is urgent that I speak to him." pages the Mayor. "Yes sir, right away sir." replies Alice. "Mayor Ferguson I have Governor Grahm on line one," pages Alice. Mayor Ferguson picks up line one on the speaker phone, "Yes sir, I am here with FBI Special Agent Mr. David MacQuire. We are about to hold a press conference and I wanted to fill you in beforehand. The FBI has uncovered fifty years of unnoticed child abuse, neglect, sexual abuse, rape, and murder at the hands of the staff of Pays des Belle Haute Children's Home. One of which is a serial pedophile turned serial killer; how he got hired is unknown. Senior local officials are also involved as well; a local Priest and two Nuns, a Police Officer, the Chief of Police, and a Senator. I am sure you are aware of Senator MacKenzie's involvement since it has been on the news. Every suspect involved has been apprehended by the FBI. A medical examiner has examined all of the children, and the custody of the children has been turned over to DCFS. DCFS has picked up the children and taken them to safety. The FBI has uncovered a total of sixty nine remains at the Children's Home. One of which was Mr. Bud Dyer the Headmaster, another was his daughter Sarah, and my sister Darla. The death toll of sixty nine is due to slightly increase after DNA testing is completed on found cremated remains. Also, Governor, the FBI has uncovered that the Children's Home has been illegally operating a crematory device without State and Federal License or Permit. The FBI has helped the Pays des community uncover the truth, bring an end to the sadistic murder and abuse of innocent children, and also help bring closure to many families including my own." states Mayor Ferguson. "Well Mayor Ferguson sounds like you have everything under control there. Thank you for filling me in and letting me know. Just let me know if there is anything I can do to help your community. And Mayor Ferguson, my thoughts and prayers to you and your family." responds Governor Grahm as he hangs up his line.

"Well Special Agent MacQuire are you ready for this." asks Mayor Ferguson. "As ready as I'll ever be." says David. They get up walking together out to the podium where dozens of news media have been patiently waiting. As they approach the podium cameras begin radically clicking, and bright flashes flashing with each camera click echoing throughout the room. Mayor Ferguson walks up to the microphone, "Good afternoon. I know that you all, like me, have been wondering just what has been going on in the Pays des community these past few days. First Senator MacKenzie is arrested, and then the Chief of Police. The Headmaster of Pays Des Children's Home Mr. Bud Dyer turns up missing, and now all of the Staff of Pays des Children's Home are taken into custody by the FBI. The FBI has been conducting an investigation of the Pays des Children's Home for the past several months, and they have uncovered fifty years of unnoticed child abuse, neglect, sexual abuse, rape, and murder at the hands of the staff of Pays des Belle Haute Children's Home. One of which is a serial pedophile turned serial killer; how he got hired is unknown. This abuse was also suffered at the hands of some of our local leaders as well. The FBI has uncovered a total of sixty nine remains at the Children's Home. One of which was Mr. Bud Dyer the Headmaster, another was his daughter Sarah. The FBI has also uncovered that the Children's Home has been illegally operating a crematory device without State and Federal License or Permit. I would like to introduce FBI Special Agent Mr. David MacQuire who has been leading this investigation." states the Mayor. "Hello, as the Mayor said I am FBI Special Agent Mr. MacQuire in charge of this investigation being conducted by my team of experts. As I have told the Mayor the FBI has not come to the Pays des community to wreak havoc and devastation. We are here to help the community uncover the truth, stop the sadistic murder and abuse of innocent children, and to help bring closure to many families. I will now turn back over to Mayor Ferguson." responds David. The Mayor steps up to the microphone, "We will now answer any questions you may have." states the Mayor.

"Yes Mayor Ferguson I am Rob editor of "Ye Ole Town Paper," sir just what leads you to believe that any abuse at the Pays des Children's Home has been going on for fifty years from just a two month investigation, and what proof do you have?" questions Rob. "I will redirect that question to Special Agent Mr. MacQuire." replies Mayor Ferguson. David steps up to the microphone, "Well as you know the Pays des Children's Home was founded fifty years ago by the local Catholic diocese, and shortly sold to private enterprise. The Maintenance Garage back then was a barn with dirt flooring, and the basement of the Children's Home was also dirt flooring with wooden steps leading down to the basement. There was a coal furnace in the cellar. When the private enterprise took over Pays des Children's Home they built a new Maintenance Garage, with cement flooring. They also rebuilt the basement of the Children's Home with cement steps leading down to cement flooring in the basement. They also replaced the coal furnace with a small crematory device. During the process of recovering buried remains we found buried remains under the cement flooring in the Maintenance Garage; as well as, under the cement flooring in the basement," responds David. "So Special Agent MacQuire, a couple buried remains recovered under the cement from way back then constitutes abuse?" asks Rob. "No sir, I did not say that we found a couple buried remains from fifty years ago. We found ten buried remains under the cement from fifty years ago, and we will not know how many illegally cremated remains from way back then until after my team is done with DNA testing of the cremated remains." responds David.

"Special Agent MacQuire, Julie from KSAP News, just how abusive can a couple of Nuns be?" asks Julie. "Well Julie, unless any further evidence is produced; the two Nuns will be charged with Educational Neglect, Medical Neglect, and Psychological Child Abuse," replies David. "Also Special Agent MacQuire, the Children's Home was scheduled to become the new Regional Youth Detention Center with a 2.5 million dollar funding package to build a new annex; what will become of that?" asks Julie. "Well Julie, all I can tell you is that the FBI has seized any and all assets concerning the Children's Home." replies David. "So what you are saying is that there won't be a Regional Youth Detention Center now," asks Julie. "No, I did not say that Julie, what I said was there will not be a Regional Youth Detention Center built with these frozen assets." replies David.

"Mayor Ferguson, Daniel with "Lighthouse Press," is it true that this investigation brings closure to you and your family with your sister being found and how are you taking it?" asks Daniel. Mayor Ferguson steps up to the microphone, "Well Daniel I guess no differently than any other family. For the past three years my family and I have been taking each day, one day at a time. Hoping and praying that one day my sister will be found. Now that she has been found we can thank God, and give her a proper loving family burial she deserves." replies the Mayor.

"Mayor Ferguson, Steve from "Pays des Reporter," what is going to happen now with the children at the Children's Home?" asks Steve. "I will redirect that question to Special Agent Mr. MacQuire." replies Mayor Ferguson. David steps up to the microphone, "Yes, after my team finished assessing each child's immediate medical needs, recommended treatment, and gathering each child's statement; the custody of all of the children was turned over to the DCFS. DCFS has taken all of the children by bus to other facilities with space available. All of the children are safe." replies David.

Mayor Ferguson walks up to the podium, "Well, this concludes our report. We will keep you informed if anything new develops." states Mayor Ferguson. The Mayor and David, walk back to the Mayor's Office. "Special Agent MacQuire, I want to thank you for all of your hard work. Also for helping all of those children; like me I am absolutely positive that you also wish we could have found this out sooner. A lot of children would be alive today had we known." states the Mayor as he extends his hand to David. "Thank you Mayor Ferguson and yes I totally agree with you. Take care." replies David as he shakes the Mayor's hand.

On his way to his car, David gets out his cell phone and calls his sister's cell phone, "Hey sis, bring those two love birds home!" states David.

This Concludes the "Status Quo"

Senator Daniel MacKenzie

Convicted of - Child Neglect, Lewd Acts, Child Sexual Abuse, Aggravated Child Sexual Battery, Statutory Rape, Child Molestation, Emotional Child Abuse, and Psychological Child Abuse. Sentenced to - Life in Prison without Parole. Wife Elizabeth MacKenzie files for Divorce.

Chief of Police, Captain Briar MacKenzie

Convicted of - Child Neglect, Lewd Acts, Child Sexual Abuse, Aggravated Child Sexual Battery, Statutory Rape, Child Molestation, Emotional Child Abuse, and Psychological Child Abuse. Sentenced to - Life in Prison without Parole.

Officer Brice Reid

Convicted of - Child Neglect.
Sentenced to – 25 years in Prison without Parole.

Priest Father Mitchell Quinn

Convicted of - Child Neglect, Lewd Acts, Child Sexual Abuse, Aggravated Child Sexual Battery, Statutory Rape, Child Molestation, Emotional Child Abuse, and Psychological Child Abuse. Sentenced to - Life in Prison without Parole. The Archbishop defrocked Father Quinn, and submitted laicization to the Vatican for approval.

Sister Diane Livingston

Convicted of - Child Neglect, Educational Neglect, Medical Neglect, Emotional Child Abuse, and Psychological Child Abuse. Sentenced to – 25 years in Prison. Excommunicated from being a Nun.

Sister Patricia Reeves

Convicted of - Child Neglect, Educational Neglect, Medical Neglect, Emotional Child Abuse, and Psychological Child Abuse. Sentenced to – 25 years in Prison. Excommunicated from being a Nun.

Nurse Aileen Anderson

Convicted of - Child Neglect, Medical Neglect. Sentenced to – 25 years in Prison.

Administrator/Headmaster Tavin MacKenzie

Convicted of - Child Neglect, Attempted Murder. Sentenced to - Life in Prison without Parole.

Administrator/Headmaster Bud Dyer

Murdered by serial killer Torey Reid.

Administrator/Headmaster Secretary Christal MacKenley

No Charges pending released from custody.

Assistant Administrator/Headmaster
William MacKenley

Convicted of - Child Neglect, Medical Neglect, Murder. Sentenced to – Life in Prison without Parole.

Cook Dulcie Hayes

No Charges pending released from custody.

House Mother Colina Gaven

Convicted of – Child Neglect, Medical Neglect. Sentenced to – 25 years in Prison.

House Father Adair Anderson

Convicted of - Child Neglect, Lewd Acts, Child Sexual Abuse, Aggravated Child Sexual Battery, Statutory Rape, Child Molestation, Emotional Child Abuse, Psychological Child Abuse, and Five counts of Murder. Sentenced to – Death by Lethal Injection.

Janitor Douglas Quinn

Shot and killed in self-defense by FBI Special Agent David MacQuire.

Maintenance Technician Grounds
Keeper Torey Reid

Serial Pedophile turned Serial Killer. Convicted of - Child Neglect, Lewd Acts, Child Sexual Abuse, Aggravated Child Sexual Battery, Statutory Rape, Child Molestation, Emotional Child Abuse, Psychological Child Abuse, and sixty one counts of Murder. Sentenced to – Death by Lethal Injection.